Readers love
STEPHEN OSBORNE

Under a Blood-red Moon

"Those who gleefully devoured the four previous Duncan Andrews Thrillers will love this fifth outing and newcomers to the supernatural series will become converted to a new guilty pleasure."
—*Divine Magazine*

"Osborne writes with a wry sense of humor…"
—Prism Book Alliance

Speaking of Dreams

"This book is funny and clever and unique."
—The Blogger Girls

"I was definitely drawn into this book as soon as I started it and I could not put it down."
—Inked Rainbow Reads

Dead End

"I love scary stories and reading this one alone in the dark definitely gave me the heebie-jeebies."
—It's About The Book

"It has everything a good read needs—characters with interesting personalities, a little angsty romance, good friends, action and danger, all within a well written and paced plot."
—Literary Nymphs Reviews

By STEPHEN OSBORNE

Cuddling (Dreamspinner Anthology)
Pop Goes the Weasel • Rat Bastard
Raven's Rest
Speaking of Dreams
Temporal Driftwood
Wrestling with Jesus

DUNCAN ANDREWS THRILLERS
Pale as a Ghost
Animal Instinct
The Scarlet Tide
Dead End
Under a Blood-red Moon

Published by DREAMSPINNER PRESS
www.dreamspinnerpress.com

RAVEN'S REST

STEPHEN OSBORNE

Published by

DREAMSPINNER PRESS

5032 Capital Circle SW, Suite 2, PMB# 279, Tallahassee, FL 32305-7886 USA
www.dreamspinnerpress.com

Raven's Rest
© 2016 Stephen Osborne.

Cover Art
© 2016 Anna Sikorska.
Cover content is for illustrative purposes only and any person depicted on the cover is a model.

ISBN: 978-1-63477-700-1
Digital ISBN: 978-1-63477-701-8
Library of Congress Control Number: 2016906846
Published September 2016
v. 1.0

Printed in the United States of America
∞
This paper meets the requirements of
ANSI/NISO Z39.48-1992 (Permanence of Paper).

For Maggie Geise:
Enjoy your journey, my friend!
You are an inspiration!
Love ya!

CHAPTER ONE

THERE WAS nothing about the inn, other than its somewhat evocative name, to suggest that dark secrets were housed within. I first saw the Raven's Rest in the early twilight hours, and to me it looked like heaven. The Raven's Rest Inn gave a homey impression: a large white building, a former farmhouse that had been added on to over the years. Here, the house seemed to say, you can find peace and tranquility. It beckoned to the weary traveler, offering solace from the hustle and bustle of the city. The perfect place to get away.

And getting away was just what I needed to do.

Escape might be a more apt word.

I sat in my car in the parking lot, holding in my hand the brochure for the Raven's Rest Inn that I'd picked up at a rest stop along the highway. I'd switched the engine off, but I hesitated before getting out and going inside. There was no longer enough light to read, but I'd already perused the pamphlet enough times that I knew the basic contents by heart. The Raven's Rest boasted eleven suites, perfect for the traveling businessman or the vacationer who wanted to enjoy the sights and shopping available in the town of Banning, Illinois. I gazed out the window at the Halloween decorations near the entrance. Orange lights outlined the doorway, and a candlelit jack-o'-lantern was positioned to one side of the steps, its flame guttering slightly from the evening breeze. Fake tombstones adorned the lawn, and a white-sheeted ghost hung from the branch of a large oak tree, either welcoming guests or warning them to stay away, I wasn't sure which.

I'd first tried the Holiday Inn just off the freeway, but they were booked solid. The manager on duty had been good enough, however, to check to see if any rooms were vacant in the vicinity. Due to a last-minute cancellation, he told me, I could stay at the Raven's Rest Inn, just outside of town. He even provided me with directions. Maybe he saw something in my eyes that made him take pity on me, or maybe he was just always so accommodating.

The trouble was, this place looked like it would be a tad more expensive than a Motel 6 or the Holiday Inn. And while I had enough money in my bank account to last me a couple of months, I didn't know how long I'd have to stay at the Raven's Rest. It could be weeks, and unless they made me a deal, that might cut one hell of a chunk out of my bankroll.

On the other hand, if Kevin came looking for me, he'd never think to check this place out. He knew my frugal nature, and he'd never think of looking for me at a fancy joint like the Raven's Rest.

My heart was beating fast, and I could feel a panic attack approaching. Forcing deep breaths, I chanted, "You can do this, Michael. You can do this."

Could I? Yes, I could. I had to.

I tossed the pamphlet onto the passenger seat and got out of the car, my mind made up. After all, I was starting a new phase of my life. I might as well do things right.

Besides, I deserved a little luxury. I'd put up with Kevin for five years, hadn't I?

As I made my way to the front entrance, the inn seemed to be speaking to me, telling me I'd made the right decision. *Welcome*, an imaginary voice said inside my head. *We want you to feel like the Raven's Rest is your home. Stay as long as you like. We'll protect you.*

If Kevin really did try to find me, I'd need protecting.

The mere thought of what he'd do if he located me made my knees weak, but somehow I made it up the steps to the porch. The jack-o'-lantern grinned eerily at me.

Inside, the atmosphere was warm and friendly. The owners had gone to some pains to make the Raven's Rest look as little like an inn as possible. In many ways, I could have been walking into someone's private home. The check-in desk was small and positioned off to the side, so as to lessen its visual impact. What I saw first was a grand staircase, the banisters festooned with black-and-orange crepe paper in honor of the coming holiday, hardwood floors polished to a shine, and clean white walls with plenty of framed pictures. Most of the photographs were of the inn itself, showing it during different times in its history.

Behind the desk was a tall, thin, young black man. I myself was pretty tall, but he towered over me, so he had to be at least six foot four. And when I said thin, I meant almost skeletal. But he had a welcoming grin on his face that extended to his eyes, as if he genuinely was pleased to see me.

"Welcome to the Raven's Rest," he said. "How can I help you?"

A sudden, gripping fear seized me. Did I really have the nerve to go through with this? I knew not a soul in Banning. I had no job and no prospects. If I went back now, maybe Kevin wouldn't be too angry. True, I'd have to endure his tirades for months to come, but maybe they wouldn't be so bad.

No. A new life. A new start.

And it started here, in the Raven's Rest.

"I think they called you from the Holiday Inn, the one by the highway," I said as I approached the desk. "My name is Michael Cook."

The young man's grin spread, which I wouldn't have thought possible. "Only Holiday Inn in the area, so I hope it was them. But yeah, they called for you. We had a cancellation, so you can have the Ulalume Suite."

"Ulalume?" It sounded like an odd name to me.

"All our rooms are named after either stories or poems by Edgar Allan Poe. Guy that built this place was a bit of a Poe nut." He chuckled to himself, I think over the term "Poe nut."

"So there must be a Raven Suite, and maybe a Black Cat Suite?"

"Oh yeah. The Raven Suite's the big one on the second floor. You'll like the Ulalume, though. Nice view of the gazebo and the gardens. How long were you planning on staying, Mr. Cook?"

That was a good question. I wished I had a good answer. Should I play it safe and go day by day? No, that would be a hassle, and what if they booked someone else into the room? "Can I pay for a week up front?" I asked. "I may need to stay longer, in fact."

"Sure can." The young man did some typing on his keyboard. The homey feel extended to the staff's attire. Instead of a stuffy suit, the desk clerk was wearing a flannel shirt over his bony frame, and comfortable-looking jeans. A name tag over his left breast informed me his name was Lonnie. I decided I liked Lonnie a lot. My first friend in Banning.

The clock behind him told me that it was nearly ten o'clock, much later than I'd thought. I must have spent more time at that rest stop than I'd realized as I'd tried to figure out what I was going to do with myself for the next few days. "Sorry I'm so late," I said.

"Hey," Lonnie said, "no problem. I'm here all night."

"Good place to work?" I asked.

Now his grin showed his teeth. "I'd better say yes, since my mom owns the place."

I laughed along with him. "I guess you'd better. Business been good?"

"Real good this week, but then we've just had Banning's fall festival. Normally we wouldn't be all booked up like this."

He gave me the price for a week, which wasn't as bad as I was expecting, and I forked over my credit card. As he processed the transaction, I took in more of my surroundings. Off to the side of the staircase was an archway leading to what looked like a little gathering place for guests. Currently it was in darkness. Opposite it was a solarium, with two walls almost entirely made up of glass. Lots of wicker furniture and potted plants. Looked like a good place to read when things were quiet.

Lonnie gave me back my credit card and handed me a key card. "The Ulalume Suite is on the second floor, all the way down to the left. Do you need help with your baggage?"

"It's out in the car. I can grab it myself." One bag, in fact. Everything I now owned, reduced to one suitcase. There was a lot of shopping in my future.

What the hell was I doing? I opened my mouth, ready to hand Lonnie his key card back and tell him I'd made a terrible mistake. When I looked at him, however, he had such a friendly look on his face, I couldn't disappoint him, not to mention myself. A genuinely good soul, this Lonnie, and God knew I needed good things in my life right now.

"In town on business, Mr. Cook?"

"Call me Michael. And no, just here to see the town."

That surprised him just a little. "Not much to see in Banning. The fall festival is pretty much over. Don't worry, though. You won't get bored."

I was reluctant to leave him. After all, what would I do up in my room all by myself? Probably fret about my decision to leave Kevin and get myself all worked up. So I forced a smile on my face and leaned in closer to Lonnie, as if we were being conspiratorial. "So tell me, with a name like the Raven's Rest, is this place haunted?"

Lonnie surprised me by loudly proclaiming, "Hell, yeah! We've got at least three ghosts roaming the halls. Don't worry, though. They hardly ever visit the Ulalume Suite. Now if you were staying in the Black Cat...." He left that room and what went on there to my imagination.

"Three ghosts?" I said, letting my skepticism show.

"At least."

"Ever seen one?"

He chuckled. "Not as such. But I've had a lot of weird things happen to me, and I've seen shadows move when there isn't anyone around. Once, I saw a guy out of the corner of my eye, right there on the stairs. But when I turned to say something to him, there was no one there. Want to see him?"

Was Lonnie offering to show me an actual ghost? "See him?"

The young man emerged from behind the desk and led me over to one of the photographs on the wall. "That's him there. Coleman Hollis. He lived here around 1980 or so. His father was the guy who renovated this place and turned it into an inn."

The picture was in black and white and showed part of the grounds, including the gazebo. Standing in the structure, facing the camera, was a serious-faced young man with long blond hair. The photo was obviously meant to showcase the beautiful lawn and gardens, and Coleman Hollis wasn't the main feature. In fact, it was hard to tell much about him, other than the long hair and that he was a handsome guy.

"1980?" I asked. "I take it he died young."

Lonnie shrugged. "Actually, he disappeared. At the time, a lot of folks around here just thought he ran off somewhere. His father, Darryl Hollis, wasn't exactly a nice guy. I wouldn't say he's changed either. He still lives in town. But no one's seen or heard from Coleman for years, as far as I know. When my mom bought this place a few years ago, we started hearing from guests who claimed to see the apparition of a young man. Finally someone pointed out this picture and said it was him that they'd seen. Which tells me that Coleman didn't live long after he ran off. I guess he decided to come back home, though. In ghost form." Lonnie smiled at his macabre joke.

I shivered, even though I was still wearing my jacket. It was like the air around me had suddenly plummeted several degrees. I looked around. "There must be a draft coming through here."

"Or maybe that was Coleman, saying hi." Lonnie favored me with a sly smile. "We get cold spots a lot here, which from what I understand is pretty common in places that are haunted."

I shook my head. "You really believe that ghosts reside here, don't you?"

"Sure do." Lonnie's face turned grave. "Hey, let's keep that just between you and me, though. If my ma overheard me talking to a guest about ghosts, she'd give me one hell of a tongue-lashing. Unless they come especially because of the inn's reputation. Then it's all right. Some people do, you know. They request the rooms that have the most activity."

I chuckled. "I'm sure I'll be just as happy in the ghost-free Ulalume Suite."

For a moment I thought Lonnie was about to give me a reassuring pat on the shoulder. I wouldn't have objected. Instead he just grinned at me with that toothy smile of his. "I'll tell the spirits to leave you alone, Mr. Cook."

"Michael."

Lonnie nodded. "Michael. Hey, you need anything, you just ask."

Well, I needed a new life. I refrained, however, from letting Lonnie know that. Some things were best kept to yourself.

APPARENTLY LONNIE was doing double duty as both check-in clerk and bellboy, as he showed me to my room himself. Or maybe, at that time of night, he just didn't have much to do. I retrieved my suitcase from my car, and he led me upstairs, chatting all the way about the inn, the town, and his life in general. My mind was still pondering that sudden cold chill I'd experienced, so I only half listened to him. I learned he'd graduated from Banning High School two years previously, so he was either nineteen or twenty, and that he was dating a girl named Maria.

I noticed that the doors to the rooms had placards next to them with the name of the suite. No numbers. We had to pass the Annabel Lee and the Lenore Suites to get to our destination, and no sounds came from within. I knew the place was booked up, but so far I'd seen no one other than Lonnie, nor had I heard a peep out of another guest.

"Is it always so quiet here?"

Lonnie answered me with his customary good cheer. "Almost everyone staying here right now is with a business convention. Book publishing. The convention is actually in Rockford, but we got the overflow, I guess. Or the ones that wanted to stay in some out-of-the-way place and don't mind driving the forty miles into the city. Maybe a few of them wanted to take in some of the festival. Anyway, they're all in the city right now at their convention. Probably drinking too much and telling really bad jokes. You know how conventions are."

I didn't, but I could imagine. We arrived at the end of the hall. The placard on the wall announced that this was the Ulalume Suite. With a flourish, Lonnie opened the door and ushered me in.

If it wasn't the fanciest suite the Raven's Rest had to offer, I'd hate to see what was. To me it was amazing. The room was dominated by a huge four-poster bed, the blue covers matching the carpeting. There was a fireplace, a writing desk, and a mahogany chest of drawers on which was perched a big television. To my right was the bathroom, and through the open door I could see shining fixtures and a sunken bathtub in the corner. If I never left the room at all, I'd be happy with my stay at the Raven's Rest.

Lonnie indicated the fireplace, above which, on the mantel, was a small bust of Edgar Allan Poe himself. "This is gas. The logs are fake, of course. If you want, I can turn it on. Get rid of the chill you felt. Or I can show you how it works."

He turned it on for me as I wandered around the room, checking out the furnishings and even running a hand down the thick drapes, which were neatly tied back to allow one to see the view, which was just blackness, as it was night. Knowing Lonnie was expecting me to say something, I chuckled. "This is fantastic."

"It's something, ain't it?"

Lonnie left shortly after that, armed with a sizable tip from me. As soon as the door closed behind him, I immediately felt a pang of loneliness, or perhaps it was regret. Was I doing the right thing? Yes, I was. There was no doubt about that. *Keep telling yourself that, Michael, and maybe you'll start believing it. You had to get away. You had to leave. You had to start afresh.*

And what better place to hide myself away than Banning, Illinois? Kevin would never think of looking for me here.

Could he track me by my credit card? It was in my name only, but I wouldn't put it past Kevin to try to get the information somehow. He'd controlled nearly every aspect of my life for the past five years—since I was Lonnie's age, in fact. It wouldn't surprise me to learn that he'd memorized my credit card number. Could he call the issuing bank with some story about it being stolen, give them the number, and see if any recent charges had been made?

I didn't know if that was possible, but to my mind it seemed plausible enough that worry began to eat away at me. Kevin had never laid a hand on me, not yet, but me running out on him might change that. The thought of his reaction upon locating me filled me with dread.

Wanting to calm myself and splash some cold water on my face, I went into the bathroom. As I switched on the light, I marveled at the silence. The inn seemed so remote. Outside, there were no police sirens, no muffled voices from drunks leaving the bar that Kevin and I had lived right across the street from. I couldn't even hear any dogs barking. It was almost eerie, the quiet. I wasn't used to it.

After I washed my face and took a few deep breaths, the panic attack that had been threatening to seize me abated a little. If Kevin found me, I'd deal with it. I was an adult, and he had no hold over me. I could do whatever I wanted. He couldn't make me go back with him. Oh, he'd yell and call me names, but nothing he could do would convince me to go back to Rockford. I had no friends who would miss me. All the people I knew were Kevin's friends. I'd made my decision.

I dabbed at my face with the washcloth and examined myself in the mirror. I liked what I saw. Okay, I wasn't model material. Abercrombie & Fitch weren't going to be banging at my door, beseeching me to pose for their latest ad. But hey, if you were into the gay geek look, I was your guy! Thin, with long brown hair (okay, it could use a trim… and maybe a style) and intelligent-looking hazel eyes and a sense of fashion (geek chic), I was pleased with my features. I truly was.

Which, for someone who'd been in a verbally abusive relationship for half a decade, was a step in the right direction.

The trouble with someone constantly telling you that you're stupid or silly-looking or whatever is that, after a while, you begin to believe it. Or at least I did. Kevin had me convinced that if I ever left him, I'd never find love again. No one else would want me. I was absentminded. My red-framed glasses (admittedly large for my face) made me look like a weird sort of bug. I couldn't cook worth a damn. (Okay, he might have had a point there.)

Ah, and I was a lousy lay. Couldn't forget that one.

Well, Kevin Alexander, that was the old Michael Cook. The new Michael Cook knew that he was smart, that he was good-looking, and that there were other people out there who could fall in love with him.

I gripped the edge of the bathroom counter until my knuckles turned white. "Oh please," I said to a God I wasn't sure existed, "let me get through this. If you can guide me through two days, I'll take it from there." What was it, Monday? Yeah. "Just help me along until Wednesday. After I've got a few days under my belt, the fear will ease up enough, and I'll know I can make it."

I couldn't go back to Kevin with my tail between my legs, begging for forgiveness. I just couldn't.

"Bryan."

I blinked, certain that I'd heard someone speaking, saying a name. It sounded so close, I glanced over at the shower curtain, sure that someone was lurking behind it. "Hello?" I said aloud. "Anyone here?"

I walked out of the bathroom, certain that Lonnie had returned and had gotten my name wrong. No one was there. Sure that I'd heard a voice, I even opened the closet and peered in there. No, I was alone in the room. Maybe it was one of the ghosts Lonnie had told me about. I chuckled to myself and went over to the bed.

Sitting on the edge, I removed my shoes and massaged my feet for a moment. I'd imagined the voice, of course. I was just nervous. It was my first night away from Kevin. Naturally I was going to be jumpy.

I lay back on the bed, which was wonderfully firm and warm. Would I be able to sleep? I was exhausted, true, but that didn't always mean I could sleep. Maybe I could find some boring movie on television to help lull me off to dreamland.

Something cold touched my cheek. It felt like icy fingers brushing my skin. The sensation lasted a mere second, but it was enough to make me jump to my feet, sure that someone was behind me on the bed.

Of course no one was there.

Lonnie's stories of ghosts had fueled my imagination. That was all.

I couldn't shake the feeling, however, that I wasn't alone in the room.

Chapter TWO

I SLEPT fitfully, even though an old *Thin Man* movie did its best to induce sleep. After a morning shower, I decided to take a walk around town and see just where I'd settled myself. It had been too dark when I'd arrived last night to really get an idea of what Banning had to offer, so I donned some jeans, a pastel blue T-shirt, a blue button-down shirt over that, and a canary yellow sweater (I liked layers) and went out for my stroll. I wore my black canvas basketball shoes, the ones Kevin hated, just to spite him. He'd always said they were a stupid purchase. "Only kids and young guys refusing to admit they're not kids any longer wear those," he'd said on more than one occasion. *Well, you know what, Kevin? Fuck you!*

Lonnie wasn't at the front desk. Instead there was an older black woman. I assumed this was his mother. She greeted me cordially and called me by name, even though I'd never seen her before. Well, with eleven rooms it probably wasn't hard to learn each guest's name. There were several people enjoying coffee and donuts in the solarium. They all seemed to know each other, so I guessed they were all part of the business conference.

Outside, the weather was chilly but not bad. The air was crisp and the sun was shining. Not bad for Day One of my new life.

The Raven's Rest was on the edge of town, so I turned right, intending to stroll down to the main thoroughfare. If I remembered correctly from my drive into town, I had several blocks to walk before getting to Washington Street, but time wasn't pressing on me.

I'd done a search on my laptop while watching TV in the admittedly comfortable bed and learned that Banning had a population of 4,300. Not exactly a metropolis. It was located on the Rock River and was in Ogle County. In the old days, the Potawatomi and Winnebago Indian tribes had held this land,

and apparently there were still burial mounds to be found in the area. Great. Didn't they say Indian burial grounds helped spur supernatural activity? I was only about forty miles away from my home in Rockford, which surprised me. It seemed like I'd driven farther than that, but then I'd made lots of stops and hadn't exactly made a straight journey. I'd driven in circles, trying to decide what to do and where to go.

And I'd ended up here, in this quaint little town in an inn inspired by a writer of creepy tales. Home now, at least for a while.

I knew I should be coming to Washington Street soon, and I knew from my arrival that I'd find most of the businesses and shops along there, but I was feeling hungry, so I found a little diner and went inside. The sign outside told me that this was the Coffee Cafe and that everyone was welcome. Encouraging sign. I liked encouraging signs. Another told me they served breakfast and sandwiches for lunch. I envisioned some motherly type as my waitress, who would call me "hon" and dispense worldly wisdom.

The Coffee Cafe was just what I expected—small and cozy, with tables scattered haphazardly around the room, covered with white-and-red checkered tablecloths. Most of the tables were occupied by farmer types who were probably taking a break from their morning chores to suck down some caffeine before heading back out to the fields. Or maybe they were just townsfolk enjoying some breakfast, and I was romanticizing the farmer thing.

As I sat down at the closest available table, I noticed a young man sitting near the back counter, strumming a guitar. He was dressed all in black—T-shirt, jeans, socks, and sneakers all the same shade. Even his long hair was black. He was too engrossed in his playing to have noticed my entrance, and the woman behind the counter scowled at him when he continued to strum.

"Trey! You've got a customer!"

The young man ceased his playing and looked up in surprise. "I guess I do." Reluctantly he set the guitar against the wall and rose. With a smile on his face, he approached my table. "Sorry about that. I was in another world." Not a motherly type, but I wasn't about to complain.

"A nicer one than this one, from the sound of it."

He seemed to like that comment. "Hey, can I get you a menu? Or do you know what you want?"

What did I want? Well, I never wanted to see Kevin again. I wanted to start living again. Would those things be on this magical menu? "I'll just have some scrambled eggs, some bacon, toast, and a coffee, if that's possible."

Trey grinned. "Not only possible but probable. I'll have that out for you in a moment."

I'd brought my Samsung tablet along with me, and I fired it up so I could read while I ate. Trey wasn't kidding about my food arriving quickly. I'd barely read a paragraph before he returned with a tray. As he set the plate in front of me, he eyed the tablet. "What are you reading?"

I was sure I flushed a little with embarrassment. "Um… believe it or not, *Harry Potter and the Goblet of Fire*. I've been rereading them." I wasn't sure why I was hesitant to reveal that I was reading one of the most popular books ever written. Maybe it was because I'd been a kid when I'd first read them, and now I was an adult who was finding out that he still loved them.

I shouldn't have worried. Trey nodded eagerly. "Oh yeah? They're great, aren't they? Have you read Philip Pullman? The *Dark Materials* trilogy?"

Oh my God, Trey was a reader. Beautiful, and he read. "No," I said, "but I've heard of him. I've been planning on getting his books soon."

"You should. They're fantastic."

After making sure I had everything I needed, Trey went back to his guitar, although I would have been just as happy if he'd stayed with me while I ate. As it was, I found it hard to concentrate on J. K. Rowling's words. My gaze kept straying over to the young man with the long black hair. He was slouching in his chair, his dark locks sometimes obscuring those gorgeous eyes (which were pale blue) as he looked down to find the right chord. I got the impression from his starting and stopping that he was composing something, creating a new song right there as I ate. None of the other diners seemed to mind his strumming. Maybe they were used to it.

I dawdled over my breakfast, and by the time I took my last sip of coffee (which Trey had refilled twice), nearly all of the other tables were empty. Only one guy and I were left, and he was perusing the local newspaper, every now and then sharing remarks with the lady behind the counter. He called her Gloria. She emerged occasionally to clear a table, glaring at Trey as she did so. I gathered busing the tables was his job, and he was neglecting his duties to concentrate on his playing.

Trey seemed to be adding words to his tune, and he sang as he plucked the strings. His voice was thin and reedy, but it suited the tune. I couldn't hear all the words, as he was singing quietly, but I caught enough to know it was a love song. A love gone bad. The story of my life. Every now and then I'd catch a line or two.

"It's a small town, baby," Trey sang, "but why'd you have to give me these small-town blues?"

The woman, Gloria, seemed like she wanted to give him something, namely a smack. She'd been wiping some gunk off a recently vacated table, and she turned to him, hands on her hips. "If the next Bruce Springsteen is quite finished, maybe he could start on that stack of dishes in the back."

"Almost done."

"I'll give you almost done. Trey Ramsey, you're the laziest son of a bitch I've ever known. Now get to work."

Trey looked up at her with a cheeky smile. "I'm not lazy, I'm inspired. Honestly, I've got to get this last verse fixed in my head. Then I'll get to work."

Gloria sighed with exasperation. "Okay, but just make sure everything is ready by the time the lunch crowd gets here."

"Sure thing, Ma."

So Gloria was his mother. That explained why she was putting up with his procrastination. She went back behind the counter and through a door to the kitchen area. Trey saw that I'd followed their conversation and winked at me.

"Some people just don't understand artists," he said. I gathered from his tone that he was gently mocking himself, as if he didn't think he deserved the title of artist. I begged to differ.

"I liked what I heard," I told him. "It was lovely."

"Yeah? You think? I've been saving my dough, and when I get a few more songs ready, I'm going to book some studio time and record them."

I smiled. "I'd buy it." Was I flirting? Oh my God, I was flirting!

But why shouldn't I flirt? I was single now, after my emancipation from Kevin.

Trey leaned back in his chair so that it was perched precariously on only the back legs and gave his guitar a few more strums. "Better than the last piece of shit I wrote, anyway. Had a great title, just didn't come together, if you know what I mean."

"What was the title?"

"The Penis Conversations." His eyes were twinkling, and his smile was crooked as he waited for my reaction.

I laughed. I hadn't done much laughing lately, and the sound almost frightened me. I cut it off and said, "That's some title."

"Yeah, well, the little bugger has a lot to say." Trey moved the guitar aside so he could look at his own crotch. "Don't you, you bastard?" He propped the guitar against the wall and settled the chair back down on four legs. "Anyway, it was a song about my last boyfriend and how he fucked me over." Trey emphasized the last three words, even adding syllables to the word *fucked*.

Beautiful. Gay. A musician. And he read. I'd have to stay away from Trey Ramsey or I'd fall in love with him, and falling in love wasn't on my list of things to do, not for a long time yet.

His mother returned from the kitchen, looking harried. Still with the rag in her hand that she'd used to mop the tables, she pointed at Trey. "Work," she said. "Now."

Trey winked at me again as he stood up. Turning to his mother, he presented an attitude of mock obeisance. "I'm all yours, milady."

"Well, milady requests that you wash those dishes and help her get lunch ready."

"When are you going to hire another slave?" he asked as he reluctantly made his way back to the kitchen area.

"When I can find someone fool enough to work here," she replied.

I found myself raising my hand as if I was a kid in a classroom. "I'll take a job, if you're serious."

Both Gloria and Trey turned to stare at me. "You're joking, right?" Gloria asked.

"Not really. I could use a job."

It was true. I had some savings, but extra cash could come in handy. Plus, I didn't know how long I could stay at the Raven's Rest. I'd have to start searching for a place to live if I was going to make Banning my home.

Gloria Ramsey broke into a smile. "When can you start, and what's your name, you angel?"

Chapter THREE

By lunchtime I was feeling pretty good about this new life. I was now employed—on a part-time basis—and now that I'd seen it in the light of day, I decided I liked the town of Banning. Granted, there wasn't a lot to it. It boasted only three fast-food chains, which was probably a good thing, but there were several little mom-and-pop places to make up the difference. Mainly pizza joints. Apparently Banning liked its pizza.

The county courthouse, which was on the main drag of Washington, was quaint and lovely. A sign informed me that, every weekend during the summer, there was a farmer's market on the sidewalks surrounding the building. In my wanderings I counted five bars, although there could have been some I missed, an ice cream shop, two hair stylists, and three car repair shops. Banning had three gas stations, two drug stores, and only one supermarket. The town also had one of the biggest liquor stores I'd ever seen. It wasn't hard to guess what the main source of entertainment was in town: drinking yourself into a stupor.

I found a bank and opened an account there, although I kept a little bit of money in my old account. I didn't know why. Maybe part of me still wasn't sure I wouldn't be returning to Rockford.

I chose the town's McDonald's for lunch, although I wasn't a fan of their food. To me, everything there tasted the same, but I was craving a burger, and I figured it was a safe bet. At least I knew what I'd be getting. As I ate, I recalled filling out my employment papers as I sat staring off into space. When it came to putting down my address, I'd hesitated.

Gloria Ramsey had been sitting with me, and she saw my discomfort. Patting my hand, she said, "Just put your old address down for now. Until you find somewhere new. Or list the Raven's Rest as your residence. It doesn't really matter to me. Honey, you've got the job anyway!"

In the end I'd put down the Raven's Rest, unable to acknowledge my previous residence with Kevin.

I'd offered to start immediately, but Gloria insisted I wait until Friday. "Take a few days to settle in. Then come in bright and early Friday morning, and I'll have Trey show you the ropes." She'd then rolled her eyes heavenward. "Although, truth be told, you probably should show them to him."

The thought of working alongside the beautiful Trey, I had to admit, was a pleasing one.

I'd finished my burger and was slowly making my way through the rest of the fries. The restaurant wasn't terribly busy, as it was nearing two o'clock. The employees outnumbered the customers two to one, and they were enjoying their downtime by joking while doing the minimum of chores.

The pretty girl manning the cash register was flirting with one of the boys, batting her eyes at him whenever she had the opportunity and blushing when he teased her. I half listened to their banter as I wondered what I was going to do with the rest of my day. In just a few hours I'd pretty much seen the entire town of Banning. I could always take my car and check out some of the neighboring towns and see what they had in store for me, or I could lounge around my room at the Raven's Rest, watching a movie or reading.

J. K. Rowling won out. Reading it was.

Just as I was slurping up the last of my Coke, I heard the counter girl say, "Oh my. Here comes Miss Crazy."

I followed her gaze and saw a woman coming up to the side entrance. She was middle-aged, with red hair streaked with gray. To me she looked sane enough, although she was wearing a big, bulky Christmas sweater with reindeer on it and it was only late October. Once she was inside, I also saw she had big hoop earrings and a button pinned to her sweater, a white one with black letters. The words read "The Town Witch." With a vacant expression on her face, she approached the counter and gave her order. I smiled as I watched the counter girl. She carried out the transaction carefully, as if she was afraid a sudden movement might make the redheaded woman explode.

The woman with the pin proclaiming she was the town witch sat down at the table next to me. On her tray was a small coffee and a large order of french fries. No burger. She sat and immediately popped a fry into her mouth. As she chewed, she eyed me suspiciously. She swallowed slowly and then leaned forward.

"I know you, don't I?"

I shook my head. "Just arrived in town yesterday."

She didn't seem convinced. "Nevertheless, I know you."

Maybe the counter girl had been correct in her assessment of this woman's mental state. "I don't think so," I said.

She shrugged as she ate another french fry. "Maybe not. I'm Jesenia, by the way. Jesenia Maupin."

"That's a lovely name. I'm Michael Cook."

Jesenia narrowed her eyes at me. "Always Michael, isn't it? Never Mike."

It was true I preferred Michael, but that didn't prove she had psychic powers. I smiled and said nothing. Maybe it wasn't a good idea to get into a conversation with this woman.

She didn't seem deterred. "I've seen you before, though. Maybe not in this life. But your aura is familiar."

I chuckled. "Hopefully it's a nice aura."

"It is."

I was done with my meal, so I stood and gathered up my trash. I had to pass her table to get to the waste receptacle, so I bowed slightly and said, "It's been good to meet you, Jesenia Maupin."

She sipped a little coffee and motioned for me to stop. "Let me see your hand."

"I beg your pardon?"

"I need to see your hand."

I should have kept on moving, but she intrigued me, so I set my tray down on her table and showed her my left hand.

"The right one, please." She turned it palm upward.

"You're a palm reader?" I asked.

"I'm many things," she said, tapping her Town Witch pin with her free hand. She held my hand closer to her face and frowned. "Long life line. That's good." She ran a finger across my skin. "You've faced hardship. Recently. There's a split here."

Well, that was interesting. I didn't put any faith in palmists or psychics or pretty much any New Age malarkey, but I had to admit she'd hit a nerve there. "What else do you see?"

"There's love in your future. A good love, not like the one you've known."

A chill ran down my spine. How could she possibly know that my relationship with Kevin wasn't a healthy one? It couldn't be in the lines on my palm. She had to have picked up on my body language or something. Some subtle hints my facial expression gave, or the way I stood, or whatever. Still, I hoped she was right. I immediately thought of Trey Ramsey.

"Is there a name written there?" I asked her jokingly.

The hint of a smile played on her lips. "If only it worked that way." Her face grew grave as she examined my hand further. "There's danger for you in the near future. Someone is going to try to kill you."

I had been wondering when she'd wander off into the land of dramatics. I pulled my hand away. "So now I'm supposed to get scared, and you'll offer to read your tarot cards for me or gaze into a crystal ball. For a fee, of course. And I'll be a few dollars poorer and none the wiser. Sorry, Mrs. Maupin, but I wasn't born yesterday."

She arched an eyebrow at me. "Jesenia, please. And it's Miss Maupin, anyway. But for your information, Mr. Cook, I don't charge for readings. Ever. It's a gift I sometimes share with those I like, but I never profit from it. If you would like to learn more—for free—I believe that a tarot reading would be useful. Here, take my card. You may have use for it."

She fished a business card out of her pocket and handed it to me. It was black in color with white lettering. A full moon was depicted on it, overlooking a barren landscape. Jesenia Maupin: Psychic, Palmist, Tarot Reader.

Not wanting to cause a scene, I shoved the card into my back pocket, fully intending to toss it into a trash can later. "Thank you," I said. "I'll bear that in mind."

"I'm not really a witch, Mr. Cook," she said. She waved a hand toward the McDonald's employees. "That's just what the kids in town call me, but I'm certainly not a Wiccan. Wiccans don't believe in the devil. I do. I know for a fact that he exists. Evil exists, and it resides here in Banning."

Okay, creepy. I had no doubt that she was sincere, though. I didn't get the vibe that she was a charlatan out to make a quick buck. And in a weird way, I liked her. She was strange, but she seemed genuinely concerned over my welfare, a man she'd just met minutes ago. "I have the feeling we'll meet again, Jesenia," I said.

"We will, Michael. May I call you Michael?" She smiled when I said yes. "I think we're going to be friends. Keep my card with you. You're going to need it. Don't throw it into the trash in your room at the Raven's Rest."

"How did you know I was staying at the Raven's Rest?"

Jesenia Maupin grinned. "The first word after my name on the card, Michael. Have a good day."

Psychic. I walked out of the restaurant deep in thought, pondering my chat with Jesenia. She'd certainly been right about a few things, but they could just as easily have been good guesses. The part about someone trying to kill me was ludicrous, however. I knew practically no one in Banning, and Kevin, for all his many faults, wasn't the killing type. Controlling, manipulative, demanding, yes, but physically dangerous? No.

Not paying attention to where I was walking, I nearly barreled into someone in the parking lot. The older man was just getting out of his car and had to back up suddenly to avoid colliding with me.

"Excuse me," I said, and I started to walk on, but the look on his face stopped me in my tracks. The man was maybe in his sixties or early seventies, with a jowled face and grizzled black hair liberally sprinkled with gray. There was shock in his eyes, more than you might expect from someone you nearly bumped into.

"You," he said in awe.

"I'm sorry," I said, somewhat confused. "I wasn't watching where I was going."

The man shook his head. "It's okay. It's just that—" He narrowed his eyes suspiciously at me. "You remind me of someone I used to know. Your last name isn't Finn, by any chance?"

"No, it's Cook."

Some of the worry went out of the man's face. "My mistake. Sorry."

He turned and made his way into the McDonald's. At the door, however, he glanced back at me. I could tell he was still perturbed by our encounter.

"Maybe," I said to myself as he disappeared inside, "I picked the wrong town to settle in."

BACK AT the inn, Lonnie was in charge of the front desk, and he grinned at me as I came in. "Mr. Cook, how are you doing today?"

"I'm good, Lonnie. Yourself?"

"Peachy. Been out seeing the sights of Banning? All two of them?"

I nodded. "Not exactly a booming town, is it?" The inn seemed quiet, and I noticed that the solarium and the common room (as I'd dubbed it in my mind) were empty. "The business people all out at their conference?"

Lonnie shook his head. "They've all checked out. It's just you and a couple of other people right now. We'll have a few more joining us this weekend, though."

"That's all right. I like quiet." And I believed I did. I just wasn't used to it. I stopped when I got to the bottom of the stairs and looked back at him. "What's a good place around here for dinner?"

"Alfanso's, if you like Italian."

"Alfanso's it is, then. And I don't suppose you know of any apartments that are available for rent."

Lonnie smiled. "Tired of us already?"

"Well, I'm thinking of settling here in Banning. I'll have to find a place to live if that's the case."

"The Jefferson Apartments are pretty good. They're right up the road on—"

I laughed. "On Jefferson Street." I'd already figured out that most of the roads in Banning were named after presidents.

UP IN my room, I was pleased to find that the chairs placed before the fireplace weren't as uncomfortable as they looked. I sat in one, enjoying the feel of the gas fire, and immersed myself in the world of Harry Potter.

I had just turned the page to begin chapter seventeen when I realized several things. One was that Rowling was such a good writer that I hadn't thought about Kevin for over an hour, nor had I fretted over my decision to leave him. The second thing was that it was getting late, and I was hungry. The sun had set, but I'd turned on several lamps in the room to dispel the shadows. I shut off my tablet and set it on the table next to me, then removed my glasses so I could give my eyes a good rub. Just as I retrieved my spectacles from my lap, I heard a whisper coming from behind me.

"*Bryan.*"

Certain that someone had somehow crept into my room without my knowledge, I twisted in my chair to look. There was, of course, no one there.

But I'd heard the name. It hadn't been the wind outside, or a creak of a floorboard, or water rushing through pipes in the wall. It had been a voice, a desperate voice, full of longing and misery.

"Hello?" I said to the empty room.

It didn't answer.

Feeling slightly foolish, I tried again. "My name is Michael. Michael Cook. Are you looking for someone named Bryan?" My heart was beating fast, but I wasn't scared. Excited, yes. Intrigued for sure. But I felt no threat.

I got no verbal response, but the air around me seemed to get colder. I shivered and rubbed the goose pimples on my arms. As I did so, the lights dimmed in the room. Just enough to be noticeable. Something or someone was trying to get my attention.

"I'd like to help you, if I can." My voice was hushed, partially from the sense of unease I was feeling, but also because I didn't want to alarm my unseen visitor. Although, truth be told, they were alarming *me*. Suddenly I felt the need to urinate, but my legs didn't seem to want me to rise out of my chair.

Then I saw the figure. Well, a partial figure. It was mostly a white mist. I put my glasses back on to get a better look. A white fog, vaguely human shaped, was hovering near the door to my room. Inside the mist, I could see a face, there one moment and gone the next. When it was at its most defined, I could tell it was a young man, late teens or early twenties. He had sad eyes (the colors were too muted to be able to see if they were green, blue, or whatever) and long blond hair. Strangely, his eyebrows were the most distinct feature I could see. They stood out, dark blond against misty white skin that was there and not there at once. There was just the hint of a smile on the lips when I could see them, an unhappy smile. Wishing for things that maybe had been but never would be again.

When I looked into those eyes, I felt a sorrow that made my heart feel like lead in my chest.

"Please tell me how I can help you," I said, my voice shaking.

For an answer, the figure seemed to melt into the door.

I took a deep breath and tried, unsuccessfully, to calm my nerves. Part of me wanted to scream. I could feel the hairs on the back of my neck bristling, and my gooseflesh threatened to have gooseflesh of its own. As frightened as I was, though, I felt the figure wanted me to follow it out into the corridor.

I got to my feet, my legs shaking a little. The lights had come back up, but I barely noticed as I walked over to the door. The doorknob, when I twisted it, was ice cold.

Out in the hall, I found the lighting had been muted once more. Perhaps the ghostly figure was drawing energy from it. I found the corridor eerily silent, and my hopes that someone else—anyone else!—would be wandering out of their room so they could see the specter as well were immediately dashed. The Raven's Rest was deathly quiet.

The figure was now standing outside the room that Lonnie had told me was the Raven Suite. It appeared to be waiting for me to join it, but when I took a few tentative steps, it vanished completely.

I froze, uncertain as to what I should do. I considered yelling for Lonnie so I could tell him what I'd just witnessed, but something told me that my experience was not over yet. The figure wanted me to go into the Raven Suite. I don't know how I knew that, but the sense that I should go inside was overwhelming. Slowly, I approached the room's door.

Once again, the knob was cold to the touch. I turned it slowly, wondering if the room was occupied.

The door shouldn't have opened, of course. I didn't have the proper key card, and the tiny green light that told a person that the lock was disengaged wasn't lit. But the door slowly creaked open.

I stepped inside and entered another world.

That was how it felt, anyway. It was almost like I was entering a dream, but not my own. The room was entirely different from mine and seemed furnished not as a room in an inn but as someone's bedroom. There were posters on the wall, and a writing desk piled with books and papers and an old electric typewriter. Clothes were littered on the floor, and I could see into the open closet, which was filled with more clothes hanging from the rod. On the floor under the shirts and pants were several pairs of shoes: mostly big, bulky basketball shoes. I noted that one of the posters was of Boy George, the words Culture Club written across the bottom in big bubble letters.

The bed was unmade, and there were two people on it, squirming and writhing on top of the sheets. I could see them clearly, although they seemed unaware that they were being observed. The guy on top was my blond specter, and he was bestowing desperate kisses onto the lips of the other guy, who was mostly in shadow. Both were naked, and I could see the blond guy's erection pressing against the leg of his companion as they made love.

The blond suddenly broke off the kissing and raised his head so he could gaze into his companion's eyes. Breathlessly he said, "I want to fuck you so badly."

"Should we be doing this?" the other man said. The voice seemed strangely familiar. "What if your dad—"

"Dad won't be home for hours. We've got time. Come on. I want you so fucking bad."

The other guy smiled. I sensed the grin more than saw it, as his face was still shielded from view by the pillow and the shadow the blond guy's face was casting. "Yeah," he said. "How bad?"

The blond snarled jokingly and buried his face in his companion's neck. He made noises as if he was gnawing away at the tender skin there. The two of them giggled. "Bad. Really bad," the blond said when the guffaw had died away.

"You're sure it's okay?"

"I'm sure." The young blond man sat up, and now that I could see him clearly, I saw that he was gorgeous. His eyebrows were nearly brown, leading me to wonder if he was a natural blond. His face, however, could have been painted by Botticelli, it was so angelic. Skin like porcelain, soft green eyes, and perfect red lips bent into a slight smile. "Turn over, Bryan. If I don't fuck you soon, I'm going to burst."

With a muffled laugh, his partner twisted around so that he was lying on his stomach. There was some shifting as he grabbed a pillow and placed it under himself so that his buttocks were raised. "Just be gentle, Cole. At first, anyway."

The blond, Cole, chuckled. "You like it rough, and you know it."

Bryan turned his head so that his face was away from my view. "Once we get going, yeah."

I wanted to retrace my steps, leave the room, but I was frozen in place. Whatever I was seeing, I was meant to see it. I felt, however, like a weird voyeur, spying on two people who thought they were unobserved.

But they weren't really there, of course. I was having some sort of vision. This room didn't exist, not like this. Not anymore. I was witnessing a scene from the past.

The one called Cole brought out a container of Vaseline from the nightstand next to the bed and proceeded to grease up his erect penis. He then straddled his friend's legs and got a big glob of the stuff onto his fingers. "I love you, Bryan," he whispered.

"I love you too, Cole."

Cole rubbed his Vaseline-smeared fingers along the crack of Bryan's ass, a sly smile on his handsome face. Bryan shuddered as one of the fingers found its way into him.

I tried to look away. I couldn't. "I don't need to see this," I said aloud, hoping the spirit, ghost, or whatever it was that had led me to this scene was listening. My entreaty went unnoticed.

On the bed, the two men repositioned themselves so that Cole was perched over Bryan's recumbent body. Bryan shifted the pillow beneath him to raise his ass even higher. When Cole's cock entered him, Bryan hissed and his head jerked up, finally allowing me to see his face.

It was my face.

This Bryan, whoever he was, looked a hell of a lot like me. The same unruly brown hair, although his was a bit longer than mine. The same bright hazel eyes. Same mouth. And now I knew why his voice had sounded familiar. It was the voice I'd heard when hearing recordings of myself.

Bryan—last name unknown—was me. Or at least the resemblance was strong enough that we could be twins. I looked on the nightstand. A pair of glasses had been placed there. I assumed they were his. These weren't similar to mine, as they had black frames and were of a conventional size, but I wondered if I put them on if the prescription would match mine.

Cole and Bryan's lovemaking was brief but passionate. Cole drove himself into Bryan's rear slowly at first, but soon he was fucking him with a fury driven by lust. The two were pretty vocal, and it was obvious that they'd been lovers for quite some time. They knew how to pleasure each other, knew what made the other moan and squirm. When Cole came, Bryan was no longer able to hold back his passion.

"Oh my God, baby! That feels so good!"

When they'd started, they'd obviously been trying to mute their words, talking in whispers so they couldn't be overheard. Bryan's cry as he and his boyfriend came to a shuddering climax could have been heard all over the house.

For several moments a breathless Cole lay on top of the now-sweaty Bryan, and I could tell he was drained, physically and emotionally. He whispered something into Bryan's ear that I couldn't quite catch, but the intent was clear. Words of love. Words of thanks, just for being. Words of devotion.

Outside in the hallway, there came the sound of footsteps approaching.

Suddenly Cole sprang to life. "Shit!" he said as he rolled off Bryan. He vainly attempted to cover his nakedness with the bedsheet, but it was under Bryan's body and refused to shift. The door behind me creaked open.

At that moment my head seemed to spin. The young men on the bed seemed to blur, and the room darkened. I blinked, trying to clear my head. I felt like I was swaying and my stomach was lurching.

Then everything went black.

CHAPTER FOUR

"MR. COOK, are you okay?"

Someone was shaking me, calling my name. I tried to open my eyes, but they seemed like they were glued shut. I moaned. My head hurt like hell, and I was shivering from cold. "Huh?" I said.

"I think you fell, Mr. Cook. Can you sit up?"

Who was talking? Who was clutching my shoulder? The voice sounded....

I managed to open my eyes, and once my vision adjusted to reality I could see Lonnie leaning over me. "What happened?" I asked. I was totally disoriented. Where was I? What had happened?

"You wandered into the wrong room, sir," Lonnie said. "I think you passed out."

It came back to me. The spirit leading me to this room. The vision. I even vaguely recalled blacking out. "I... saw something," I muttered. "I'm not sure what."

Slowly, I got to my feet with Lonnie's help. He had a worried look on his face. "Are you sure you're okay? You look awfully pale."

I took a deep breath and looked around me in wonder. The room was vastly different now. The bed was larger, perfectly made, and was against the other wall. There was a gas fireplace, much like the one in my room, that hadn't been there when I'd entered. No posters adorned the walls, just the sort of paintings one expects to see in hotel rooms. Even the carpeting was different. The closet had different doors and was firmly shut, but I knew that it now contained no shirts, no basketball shoes. And of Cole and Bryan, nothing remained.

Nothing except a faint whiff of cologne. No, patchouli. I'd smelled it earlier as well. Either Cole or Bryan had been doused with it. Now just the barest trace remained in the air.

"Do you smell that?" I asked Lonnie, who was still looking at me like he thought I might tumble back to the floor at any moment.

"Smell what?"

"Patchouli oil."

Lonnie sniffed the air. "I do smell something. Like a really musky perfume."

"One of them had been wearing it, or maybe they had been burning incense." I kept gazing about the room, expecting it to revert to the state it had been in when I'd first entered. Somehow this pristine room didn't seem as real as the one in my vision, which had been loved and lived in.

"Who?" Lonnie asked. He shook his head. "No one's renting this room right now, Mr. Cook. No one is staying here."

"There were two young men," I said, pointing at a spot now occupied by some chairs, "on a bed there. They were making love. One of them looked just like me."

Lonnie touched my elbow gently. He didn't want to alarm me. Didn't want to set off the crazy person. "We'd better get you back to your room, Mr. Cook. How did you get in here, anyway? Was the door left open?"

My headache was rapidly fading, and I was starting to feel more like myself. I rubbed my neck, working out some tension. "Lonnie, I'm pretty sure I've just been visited by a few of the ghosts you say have been haunting the inn. One of them was Coleman Hollis, the young man in the photo you showed me."

At first Lonnie seemed like he was going to dismiss my claim, but he examined my face carefully and sniffed the air again. The patchouli was still hanging in the air, barely detectable but there.

"Fuck," Lonnie said.

I had to agree with him. Fuck, indeed.

TREY LIT up a cigarette and took a deep drag from it, savoring the flavor.

I hadn't realized he smoked. That was a point against him. Was it enough to put me off? Probably not. Besides, he was only a fantasy potential boyfriend. I was sure he wouldn't be interested in dating. Although I seemed to have caught him looking at me in a thoughtful way several times, but that was probably just my imagination. Or me being hopeful. Or maybe I had something stuck in my teeth.

It had been his suggestion that we take a walk around town after my first shift working at the coffee shop, ostensibly to show me the sights, not that there were many. We were wandering down Orchard Avenue, a residential street, only because it had a sidewalk and there was a small park at the end of the road. "Just some grass and a bench or two," Trey said, "but it's a park."

Trey must have spotted something in my manner when he lit up. "What?" he asked, not belligerently. "Yeah, it's a bad habit, I know. Still, I gave up murder and robbing old ladies. Can't completely change overnight, you know."

I smiled. "You say that a lot."

"What?"

"You know. I know. You know?"

Trey grinned and took another puff. "Well, everyone's got to have a trademark, you know. I'm guessing yours are those bigass glasses."

It seemed like we'd been walking and talking for hours, although it could only have been about twenty minutes. As we approached West Park, which, as Trey promised, wasn't much more than some picnic tables and a swing set, I decided it was time to get back to the subject we'd been discussing on and off all day.

"So what do you think about my experience? You haven't said."

He let out some smoke. "It's trippy."

"You don't believe me."

"I didn't say that. I'm sure something happened to you. I just don't think I'm ready to jump on the ghost bandwagon."

"What else could it have been?"

"I don't know. Maybe you've got some kind of mental link with the inn, and you were seeing a scene from the past played out before your eyes. A kind of visual regression, if you will." Trey grinned wickedly. "You know?"

"Visual regression. You just made that up."

"Yup. I'm copyrighting it in the morning."

We had strolled over to the swing set, and Trey sat down, even though the spot was obviously meant for someone smaller than himself. Still, his butt was small enough he fit on the wooden perch with little difficulty. He kicked out with his feet so he could get some motion going. He smoked some more before flicking the butt into the dirt. "Thing is," he said, "I've lived in this town my whole life. Everyone knows the Raven's Rest is supposed to be haunted. Everyone. Hell, I think half the people who stay there only go because of the reputation. I've never seen anything, though."

"Have you ever spent the night there?"

"Well, no. But I've walked by it plenty of times."

"I'm sure loads of people walk by the White House and never see the President."

Trey nodded. "You've got a point there. But say we go with the ghost explanation. What do you do next?"

I looked up to the sky, as if the answers might be hanging in the clouds. "Whenever I've watched horror movies, I've always marveled at how stupid people can be. I mean, you see a ghost, you get the hell out of Dodge. Right? Leave. Go somewhere else. This is different, though. That guy, Bryan, looked like me."

"So? Doesn't mean you have to get the shit scared out of you."

"I think they're trying to tell me something."

Trey had some momentum going now, but he suddenly vaulted off the swing and landed in a cloud of dust. He brushed off his black jeans and said, "Doesn't mean you have to listen. News flash: if they are ghosts, they've been dead for some time. Even if they have something to say, it ain't going to change the fact that they're pushing up daisies. I say check out and get a room at the Holiday Inn."

I shook my head. "I don't know."

Suddenly Trey was right in front of me, and he grabbed my chin and pulled my face close to his. Before I had a chance to react, he planted his lips firmly on mine.

My shock quickly dissipated as I gave in to the moment. God, he was a good kisser. Our faces seemed to meld into one as he gently pushed his tongue into my mouth. One of us moaned. I think it might have been me. I put my arms around him, and the rest of the town, as far as I was concerned, ceased to exist. Oh sure, there were cars still driving down Orchard, and I thought there was an older woman walking a furry dog on a leash nearby, but that was another reality. The only one for me was Trey, his warm lips on mine and his thin, wiry body in my arms. Yeah, his breath tasted slightly of cigarette smoke. More than slightly. I didn't care.

Just as suddenly, Trey broke off the kiss and stepped back. He pulled out his pack of Marlboros and placed one between his lips. There was a mischievous gleam in his eyes as he flicked his lighter into action. "I think you're doing the right thing," he said. "Helping out some dead guys. Good for you."

I stared at him as he cupped the tip of his cigarette and touched it with the flame. "What was that?"

"What was what?"

"The lip-lock you just gave me."

He pocketed his lighter with a grin. "Didn't see you complaining."

"Yeah, but... what the hell!"

"You wanted to kiss me, didn't you? Or have we been giving each other the eye all morning because we had indigestion?"

I hadn't realized I'd been that obvious. "Yes, but... well, I just thought...." What did I think?

"Thought what?"

I looked around. The lady with the dog had obviously spotted our embrace, and from the look on her face, it soured her disposition. She was several yards from us, on the sidewalk along the park, waiting while the dog found just the right spot to do his business. I figured a driver or two coming along the road had also witnessed our kiss.

"I just thought if it ever happened, it might be under more romantic circumstances," I said.

Still being impish, Trey blew out some smoke and sidled up to me again. He placed a hand on my butt and pulled me to him. We kissed again, longer this time and even more passionately, if such a thing was possible. I almost could feel my heart melt.

Trey broke off the kiss and looked into my eyes. "Romantic enough for you?"

"It'll do for now," I said.

The lady with the dog *humph*ed and moved on. Her reaction seemed to please Trey. "That's Mrs. Donovan," he told me. "She used to be the town treasurer years ago, up until they discovered she was using money that wasn't hers to fund her lavish cocktail parties. So she can disapprove all she wants, fucking hypocrite."

Understanding dawned on me. "You kissed me just because she was standing there."

Trey seemed to think this over. "Yeah, I guess that was part of it. I did want to kiss you, though. Killed two birds with one stone, as they say."

It occurred to me that Trey's motives hardly mattered. I'd enjoyed the kisses and the sensations that resulted from them. I was still semihard, and if the bulge in his jeans was any indication, so was he.

For the first time in a very long time, I felt happy.

I realized I'd hardly thought about Kevin all day. Trey had dominated my thoughts, with his black clothes and his devilish smile and his pale eyes. He tried hard to put across the image that he was the town's bad boy, but I sensed that deep down he was a passionate, caring soul. At least I hoped he was.

He certainly wasn't Kevin. And that was a good thing.

While we had been washing up the dishes after breakfast, we'd briefly gone over our previous boyfriends. Trey—in his version, at least—had broken the hearts of several guys in Banning. I told him about Kevin but only in general terms. I didn't tell him that Kevin had been a controlling bastard, a verbally abusive manipulator. That was a tale that would have to wait until we were somewhere private.

Trey and I continued our walk, leaving the park and taking a bend along Orchard, past a car dealership and a women's gym. I had no idea where we were now, not that it mattered. I was with Trey, and that was all I cared about. I wasn't quite sure what about him I found so attractive. He was "pretty" rather than handsome, with his elfin features, and he was sometimes exasperating to talk to as he changed the subject often, then would go back to a previous topic as if we'd never left it. And he still lived with his mother, although he was twenty-three. Granted, it was a big house, and apparently there was a sister and a cousin and an aunt living there as well, one big happy family. Something I'd never had. He put on a show of being lazy and disgruntled, and he bragged a bit about drinking and getting into fights.

But he wasn't pushy, the impromptu kiss aside. And he was always asking what I thought, as if my opinion mattered to him. That was something new.

So far, so good.

He was wearing a leather jacket, unzipped to look cool despite the chill in the air. And he had a bit of a swagger when he walked. I wondered how much of his attitude was show and how much was real. It would be fun to find out.

Trey continued to take drags off his cigarette as we strolled along. "So are you going to ask me, or what?"

"Ask you what?"

"To come by your room tonight. I want to meet these ghosts of yours."

"I thought you didn't believe in ghosts."

"Not sure I do, but you do, so I'll keep an open mind. I like that you want to help them out. Shows a good heart."

I chuckled. "It's weird. I feel like I've known you for ages, and it's only been a couple of days."

"Maybe we knew each other in a previous life. You've obviously been here before, since Coleman Hollis was fucking you back in the 1980s."

I knew he was joking, but I wasn't sure it was all that humorous. I was born in 1990. Could I be the reincarnation of this Bryan guy? Was it possible? I had to learn more about Coleman Hollis and his boyfriend. That much was sure.

CHAPTER FIVE

"Hey, Mr. Cook! I've got something to show you."

I had now been in Banning for several days and had adjusted to a sort of routine. Thankfully, Gloria Ramsey needed a lot of help at the Coffee Cafe, and I was spending loads of time there. True, Trey's presence didn't hurt, but I'd have been glad about the job even without him, as there wasn't much to do and working there helped pass the time. I'd looked at a couple of apartments but so far hadn't found anything to my liking. Trey had promised to have the addresses of a couple of other places that were available when I arrived for my morning shift.

Despite several entreaties from him, I'd yet to show him my room at the Raven's Rest. And I couldn't really explain to Trey why I didn't invite him. I wasn't sure I knew myself. Partly I thought it was because I was afraid Trey and the room—or more precisely, the ghosts within—would clash. And I wasn't sure if I was afraid for Trey or if I was being protective of the spirits.

It amazed me that the thought of living in a haunted place didn't freak me out more than it did. Rather than frightening me, though, I found the whole thing rather like a mystery. Why were they there? What were they trying to tell me? And most importantly, why did Coleman's boyfriend look so much like me?

I was coming down the stairs from my room when Lonnie called my name and waved at me from his position behind the desk. A glance at the clock on the wall told me I had enough time for a quick chat, so I detoured over to him.

"Call me Michael," I said. "Please. Whenever you say Mr. Cook I want to look around to see if my dad is behind me." Which would have added to the inn's ghost count, as my father was no longer with us.

Lonnie grinned. "Whatever you say, Michael. Or Mike. Mikey-mike."

He certainly wasn't your typical desk clerk at an inn, but then he'd been nice to me and honored my request not to mention my incident in the Raven Suite to anyone, so I overlooked his cheekiness. It didn't hurt that his smile was infectious. "Maybe we should go back to Mr. Cook," I said.

"Sure, Michael. Anyway, I thought you'd like to see this."

He slid a book across the counter to me. It looked like a scrapbook or a photo album. I opened it to find a picture of the Raven's Rest, taken from the far end of the parking lot.

"It's an album my mom started keeping," Lonnie explained. "Pretty much everything she could find on the inn. Its history, the previous owners, whatever. See? Here's a picture from the *Banning Herald*, showing the house as it was back in the 1920s."

"A lot smaller back then."

"Yeah, you can see here where they did a lot of the adding on. That was around 1950. Here's how the house looked in 1980, when Coleman Hollis lived here."

In that photograph the house looked much more like it did now, although it lacked the additional rooms that had been added on the western end, and it had an attached garage that was no longer there. It was hard to tell from the picture, which had been clipped out of a newspaper, but I thought I could see signs of construction just at the edge of the photo. The caption read "Hollis House Renovations Underway."

"That's what Darryl Hollis was going to call it originally. When he turned it into an inn. The Hollis House. For some reason, he decided on Raven's Rest instead."

"Maybe the ghosts changed his mind," I said, only half joking.

Lonnie nodded. "Maybe. Anyway, look at this." He turned a leaf, and there was a Polaroid shot of Coleman Hollis and another young man. Coleman was sitting on a porch swing at the front of the house, and the other person was standing next to him. The colors had faded somewhat over time, but Coleman's blond hair was just as I had seen it in my vision, or whatever I'd had. He was wearing flared jeans, a white shirt, and had a beaded necklace around his neck. It appeared that the photographer had asked Coleman to smile and he'd done his best, but it was a sad smile.

My eye was drawn, though, to his companion. The young man standing was tall and thin and wore black-framed glasses. He had long brown hair that swooped over his right eye and a very serious expression.

More to the point, though, he could have been my twin.

"This is him," I said. "This is the other guy I saw."

"Look at the back of the picture," Lonnie told me.

The Polaroid was affixed to the album by notches on opposite corners. All I had to do was pluck it out. I did so and turned the picture over. There, in a faded scrawl, were the words *Coleman and Bryan Finn, 1983.*

I felt a chill across the back of my neck as I read the names aloud. "Do you know anything about this Bryan Finn?" I asked.

Lonnie shook his head. "Not a thing. Looks familiar, though, don't he?"

"He could be a relative."

"Fuck that," Lonnie said, and then his gaze darted around to make sure no one overheard his cursing. Apparently it was okay that I did. "I got a cousin, and he don't look like me. That's you, to a *T*. Okay, the glasses are different, but otherwise, it could be you."

"Except I wasn't born yet."

"Yeah," Lonnie replied, nodding sagely. "I wonder if this Bryan Finn is still alive."

"Looks like he was in his early twenties there. He'd only be, what, in his early fifties now. Do you know of any Finns in Banning?"

"Nope. And when I saw this picture, I asked Ma. She didn't either, and she knows most people in town. She said there was a Finn family years ago, an older couple, but they moved away."

"I wonder how I could find out more about this Bryan Finn. Does the local library keep old newspaper archives?"

Lonnie shrugged. "Beats me. Never been to the library here. You could try it, though."

The front door opened just then, and a woman entered. I found it hard to gauge her age. My first impression was forty, maybe forty-five, but I amended that when I saw the lines on her face and the crow's feet around her eyes and added five more years to my guess. She walked with an air of authority, and I wasn't surprised to see that under her green jacket she wore a sheriff's uniform. She strode in and nodded to Lonnie.

"Your mom in?" she asked.

"She's in the dining room."

The sheriff seemed to notice me for the first time. She arched an eyebrow and approached with an outstretched hand. "And you must be Michael Cook."

She had a firm handshake, I'd give her that. "I'm not sure it's a good thing when the town's law enforcement knows about you when you've only been in town a few days," I said.

Laughing, she explained, "I'm friends with Gloria Ramsey. She's told me all about you."

Was there that much to tell? I wondered just what my new boss had been saying. Lonnie provided the introductions. "Mr. Cook, this is Deputy Sheriff Erin Hughes."

"Pleased to meet you," I said.

"Gloria tells me you're looking for a permanent place to live here in Banning," Hughes said. "Have you checked out the Lincoln Apartments on Fourth Street? They're pretty nice, and the rates are good."

"I haven't yet, no, but they're on my list."

"Deputy Hughes's brother owns them," Lonnie informed me, "so she might be a tad prejudiced in their favor."

The deputy grinned. "Don't mean they aren't good. Well, it was nice to meet you, Mr. Cook. I'd best be heading in to see what your mom needed, Lonnie. If it's about the vandals, I hope she knows we're patrolling the best we can."

When she had left us, Lonnie explained, "We had some trouble last week with some of the neighborhood kids. Smashed our mailbox and spray painted some words on our porch."

"That explains why it looks freshly painted. What did they write?"

Lonnie smiled mirthlessly. "Hell house."

TREY AND I were finishing up the lunch dishes. He was spraying them off, and I was loading them onto the rack and then I'd shove them into the big dishwasher.

"You don't understand," I said. "He didn't just resemble me. He *was* me."

Trey looked like he was trying not to let his skepticism show too much. "So you're saying you're this Bryan guy's reincarnation."

"I don't know what to think. But if he died sometime in the 1980s, I wasn't born until 1990, so it's possible. When I met her, I should have asked Deputy Hughes if she knew about Bryan Finn."

"She's in here all the time," Trey said, rinsing off the last water glass. "You can ask her next time she's here." Handing me the glass, he yelled over his shoulder, "Ma! You ever hear of a guy named Bryan Finn?"

Gloria Ramsey was working on the books in her office space, which was really just a little area sectioned off from the rest of the kitchen by a partition. She leaned back so she could see us and thought a moment, tapping her pen against her teeth.

"Finn?" she said. "Yeah, there was a Finn family lived here years ago. I think they did have a son named Bryan. Why do you ask?"

"Michael saw a picture of him, and apparently they look alike."

Frowning, Trey's mother rose from her chair and stood leaning against the partition. "You know, I knew you reminded me of someone when I first met you, Michael. Mind you, I was just a little kid when they were around. I think I sold them some Girl Scout cookies!"

"What happened to him?" I asked.

"Bryan? Can't say as I know." She stuck the pen behind her ear. "Come to think of it, I think there was some talk around town that he'd run off with the Hollis boy. I didn't really understand it at the time, and everyone spoke about it in hushed whispers. Of course, back then two gay guys running off together was big news for a town like Banning. But this town has always lived off gossip. I think I also heard that Coleman met a girl somewhere and got married. Just shows you how many stories there are floating around this burg!"

Amanda, one of the waitresses, whom I'd worked with twice now (and whom I gathered was Trey's cousin), came back with her ticket pad, looking flustered. "We've got a late one. She just wants coffee and a scone, though, so you don't have to cook anything." She was mainly annoyed, or so I guessed, because waiting on another table meant she wouldn't get off on time and thus would be late for her movie date, which we'd heard about all morning. "And it's the crazy witch, of course, so she'll be here for ages."

"She's a big tipper, though," Trey said, attempting consolation. When Amanda's sour face didn't change, he added, "I'll bring out her stuff and clean up after her, if you want. You can go on and meet your boyfriend."

"He's not my boyfriend," Amanda protested, although you could have fooled me. The only time I'd seen a smile on Amanda's face was when she was waxing poetic about this Cody's charms. "But thanks. I'll leave you to take care of the crazy bitch."

Trey had started to get the scone and coffee ready, but I stopped him from actually taking the order out to the table. "I'll do that," I said.

He eyed me suspiciously. "This is because I said she tipped big, isn't it?"

"No," I replied with a smile. "But I'm assuming it's Jesenia Maupin, and I'd like to talk to her."

"Of course it's her. The town's only got the one crazy witch. Well, apart from my mother."

"I heard that!" Gloria had gone back to her bookkeeping, but her words sailed over the partition.

I went out into the dining room. When I set the tray down in front of Jesenia, who was wearing strings and strings of Mardi Gras beads around her neck in addition to her Town Witch button, she seemed to have been expecting me. She favored me with a sly smile.

"So how do you like your new job?"

"I'm enjoying it so far."

She looked back to the kitchen, where Trey could be heard starting the dishwasher. "It's good to have a friend, isn't it?" There was a knowing twinkle in her eyes.

"I know gossip travels fast, but I didn't realize Trey and I could be considered an item yet." After all, we'd only shared a couple of kisses. Granted, they were very public ones.

"He's a good guy," Jesenia stated simply. "He tries to be a badass, but he's really a sweetheart."

"I've gathered that." I hesitated, not sure how I should word my request. I realized that nothing I said could surprise Jesenia Maupin, so I just blurted it out. "Do you believe in reincarnation?"

"What a silly question. Of course I do." She shoved the chair opposite her out with her foot. "Sit. You and I have much to discuss."

I did as instructed, first looking back to see if Trey or anyone could see us. It wasn't that they'd mind me sitting with a customer. The Coffee Cafe prided itself on family atmosphere and being friendly, as well as being almost entirely staffed by Gloria Ramsey's relatives, so my sitting with Jesenia wouldn't bother my employer. I was more concerned that Trey might think I was being silly, which I probably was. Still, if Jesenia could provide any information, I needed to have it.

"Did you know Bryan Finn?" I asked.

My question didn't surprise Jesenia. "I was around back then, of course. But I didn't really know him. I was the same age as Coleman Hollis, though. We were at school together and shared a few classes. Bryan Finn was a year behind us."

"Do you know what happened to them?"

Jesenia cocked her head and stirred some sugar into her coffee. "According to Darryl Hollis, Coleman left after he and Bryan Finn had a big fight and eventually met some woman and got married. Bryan, legend has it, left to go after Coleman, but no one seems to know what happened to him. Neither one of them ever came back to Banning."

"But if Coleman's ghost haunts the Raven's Rest, something must have happened to them."

Leaning forward, Jesenia asked me, "Have you seen Coleman's spirit?"

There seemed little reason not to be candid. "Yes."

"Then that answers your question."

"I've seen a picture of Bryan Finn. He looks just like me."

"Which is why you were asking about reincarnation."

I nodded. "Is it possible that somehow I'm him?"

Jesenia shrugged. "Possible, yes." She pushed her tray aside, the coffee and scone untouched. From out of the pocket of her oversized sweater, she removed a deck of cards. They were larger than regular playing cards, and I recognized them at once as a tarot deck. "Are you ready for that reading I promised you?"

I wasn't sure what some cards could tell me, but I was willing to try anything. "Yes," I said.

"Shuffle the cards and tap the deck. Three times."

I did so. Jesenia proceeded to lay the cards out in a pattern. Four cards down one side and the rest in a square shape, with one card holding center court. "This card represents you."

I looked at it. "The Fool?"

"A card of beginnings and innocence." She laid a card over the Fool. I recognized it from countless horror movies. On it was depicted a skeleton in armor riding a white horse.

"Death," I said. "That can't be good."

Jesenia wrinkled her nose. "It means endings and beginnings. Change. Transformation. Don't believe what you see on TV. It's not a bad card. Not usually." She indicated another card, the top card in the cross. "This represents the path that led you to where you are today. You've had a difficult journey."

"That's an understatement."

"This card is your past."

I looked. "The Lovers. And it's upside down."

"You have ambivalent feelings about a relationship. You must listen to your heart at this time. Trust your gut. Your heart knows what is right for you, and it's important that you don't overthink the outcome." She continued with the reading, telling me what she divined through the cards and their placement. It was all pretty general, and even though there were some points that struck a chord with me, I put it down to coincidence until she came to the last card, the top of the four in the line.

"This is your outcome. The Hanged Man, reversed."

"And what does that mean? Hopefully that I escape the noose."

The feeble joke didn't amuse her. "You're at a crossroads. You must sever old ties, begin anew. The situation you find yourself in makes you want to pull up stakes and just run away. Here's what my advice is: do nothing. Stay where you are. You're here for a reason. Stick it out. There's danger ahead, and sorrow, but you must see this through."

Like astrology, I still found tarot cards a bit too broad in their meanings. Still, a lot of what Jesenia told me seemed to fit. Or was I making it fit? I sighed. "I'm not sure I have the option of giving up."

Jesenia looked up from the cards. "But you've given thought to going back to your old life. To the young man who has abused you. You shove those feelings aside, but they're there. You worry that you've made a horrible mistake and that maybe, just maybe, you should return with your tail tucked between your legs and beg forgiveness."

Okay, that was definitely more specific. I hadn't said anything to Jesenia about my life with Kevin. I let out my breath slowly. "How did you know about…?"

She smiled slyly. "It's in your aura. That, and I get further insight through the cards. They help me focus my intuition. Who is this man, the one you left?"

"His name is Kevin Alexander."

"How long were you with him?" She seemed genuinely concerned.

"Five years. He was my first love, really. And as far as abuse goes, he never laid a finger on me."

"Abuse comes in several guises." She leaned back, studying me. "I'd wager that he made you give up all your friends. You only hung out with his crowd. And he often belittled you. Made you question your self-worth."

I was suddenly uncomfortable, and I may have squirmed in my chair. "I don't really like to talk about it."

Jesenia nodded and began to pick up the cards. "Understandable. But I do have one more thing to tell you before you return to your work. I don't often get such vivid impressions from people, but I have a premonition about you."

"And that is?"

She stared at me as she returned the deck to her pocket. "You're in danger. The tarot said you should stay and see this through, but it comes with a price. Please use caution."

"That sounds… dire." I tried to sound light, but she was scaring the pants off me.

"It is." She arched her eyebrows. "Someone is going to try to kill you, Mr. Cook. I urge you to be careful. Your life may depend on it."

CHAPTER SIX

TREY WAS singing me a love song.

I noted that he couldn't look me in the eye as he played and sang in his delicate, somewhat shaky voice. He concentrated on the strings and the chord changes, but he might as well have been peering into my soul. The words were simple but, for me, powerful. Maybe it was the longing in his voice, or maybe those thin, nimble fingers moving up and down the fretboard, but I was finding it hard not to jump him right then and there and smother him with kisses.

Which would have probably shocked his mother and the few customers left in the Coffee Cafe that day.

"Haven't known you that long
Not in this life, at least
But I trust my heart
Which has sung to me the words of this song."

OKAY, BOB Dylan had nothing to worry about, but it obviously was personal to Trey, a musical confession. And I had little doubt that it was about me. As he returned to the chorus, I looked around, blushing a little. We were sitting at a table near the back counter. His mother was at the register, taking a reading of the day's take. Lonnie's mother was one of the customers, and she was listening with a thin, knowing smile as she finished her coffee.

I bit my lip. When Trey had asked me to listen to a new song he'd written, I'd eagerly agreed. I just hadn't realized that it would be something so intimate. But Trey was fond of public displays, as I'd come to learn over the past week. Most people would have waited to play me the song when we were alone somewhere. Not Trey. He had to have an audience. Like our first kiss. Maybe it was the performer in him. His life had to be witnessed.

If we were to become more than friends, I'd have to get used to that.

When the last note died away, Trey finally looked up from his guitar. "What do you think?"

What to say? I let out a breath of air slowly and then rested my chin on my hands, which were on the table. "I think you like embarrassing me."

"Well, yeah, that's a given. It's so easy. But apart from that, what do you think of the song?"

"I loved it, of course." How could you not love a song that was written for you?

Trey set the guitar against the wall. "The lyrics still need some tweaking. I'm not satisfied with them yet, but I think the chorus is there and the tune is good. The second verse sucks right now, but I sang it anyway."

"Well, I want to hear it after you've tweaked it. Probably several times."

His eyes lit up. "Yeah? Well, I'm never going to be Lou Reed, but it makes me happy."

"You've got the black clothes thing going on. The look is half the battle nowadays."

Trey slumped in his chair, suddenly seeming uncomfortable talking about himself. "People from Banning never make it to the big time, you know. It's just not done."

"You'll be the first," I said. He fidgeted more, restless, and I decided to shift the topic a little. "I'm surprised you know who Lou Reed is. I only know because my ex listened to him."

"Mom listens to all that stuff. That's where I get it from. Today's music sucks." Trey sat up straight and leaned across the table. "So how's the apartment hunting going?"

"I think I've found a place. The Lincoln Apartments look pretty good. I put an application in."

In truth, I hoped they accepted me, but I was in no hurry to move. I knew I couldn't leave the Raven's Rest until my mystery was solved. Coleman Hollis was reaching out to me. I had to know why.

Trey's eyes were twinkling. "Won't the ghosts miss you?"

I smiled. "I'm sure they will. One of them, at least."

"Any more experiences?"

"Nothing big. No visions or whispered words. But I often feel like there's someone with me in the room, and I've felt cold spots, especially near the fireplace. And when I woke up this morning, it felt like there was a hand on my chest. Like someone trying to comfort me."

"Yeah? I feel a hand that ain't there, I'm not gonna be comforted. That's for sure."

"It *was* a little unsettling."

Gloria finished with her readings and glanced briefly at her son. "Trey, don't forget to call in the supply orders before you leave."

"Yes, *mein Kapitän*!" Trey flashed his wicked grin toward me. I had grown accustomed to the banter between him and not only his mother, but all of his family members who worked at the Coffee Cafe. He waited until Gloria groaned with disgust, and only then did he get up to finish his duties for the day. As he slid his chair in, he asked me, "So what are we doing tonight? Wanna see that movie?"

We'd been discussing the latest superhero flick earlier and the possibility of driving to Sterling to see it. There were no movie theaters in Banning. "Sure," I said.

"It's a date," he said, just before disappearing back into the kitchen.

I smiled. Trey, with his black jeans and long hair, was so different from the type of guy I usually found myself attracted to. Considering my track record, though, that was probably a good thing. Kevin had been my ideal, or so I thought at the time. Handsome as hell, strong and opinionated. Quite the alpha male. A little too much so, as had become apparent. Trey was a nice contrast. He was cute and cuddly, struggling to put across the impression that he was tough.

I wondered, though, if dating right now was a good option for me. It was too soon after leaving Kevin, and my head was in an odd place. Logically, I knew I should just remain friends with Trey for now.

The heart rarely listens to logic, however. Whenever I saw that impish grin, my soul felt uplifted, reborn. Life had meaning again. And my groin agreed, and the groin was hard to argue with.

I decided, then and there, that I'd take Trey back to the Raven's Rest after the movie. And I hoped we'd find out just how good of friends we were going to be.

And in the way that the world tried to make you feel guilty for impure (but fun!) thoughts, I looked up just then to see Gloria Ramsey staring at me. She was still behind the register, seemingly lost in thought. She had her head tilted and seemed to want to say something. After a moment she picked up her ledger and the pen she'd been using and came over to my table. She nodded at the chair Trey had just vacated. "Mind if I sit?" she asked.

"Please do."

She settled herself and smiled gently at me. "You and Trey seem to be getting along rather well."

"He seems to be a nice guy."

There was a twinkle in her eye, and I knew she had concluded that Trey and I were interested in each other. "He works better when you're here. I'll give him that. Just don't start picking up his bad habits."

"I'll try not to."

Mrs. Ramsey sighed. "Are you enjoying working here, Michael?"

I felt she was beating around the bush, avoiding what she really wanted to ask. "Yes, I am." Maybe if I kept my answers short and sweet she'd get to her point.

She fidgeted, making circles on the tabletop with her forefinger. "And you're still staying at the Raven's Rest?"

She knew I was, so I merely nodded. My apartment hunting had been discussed all morning.

"That place has a reputation, you know."

"I've heard," I said.

Mrs. Ramsey sat up straight, finally ready to speak her mind. "I've heard you and Trey talking. You've had some interaction with the spirits there."

I noted that she didn't say "supposed interaction" or "spirits that are supposed to be there." As her attitude seemed friendly and welcoming rather than skeptical, I replied, "Yes. Several times now."

"Did you know that I used to work at the Raven's Rest?"

I shook my head, surprised. "Trey never mentioned it."

"It was years ago, right after it became an inn. Trey's father was still around back then. I cleaned the rooms. The owner then was a man named Nelson. He's the guy who bought it from Darryl Hollis. Anyway, it wasn't long before I began to hear the stories about the Raven's Rest. Other employees would talk, and a few of the guests. I didn't put much stock in it. Just stories. Then one evening I saw a ghost.

"I was working late. They'd had a big dinner party, a sort of murder mystery thing. Lots of people from town came. I was really just there to help serve food and to help clean up afterward. Almost everyone had gone home, and Mr. Nelson asked me to take some linens upstairs and put them in the closet at the end of the hall. I went up, as asked, but as I walked down the hall I heard some voices coming from one of the rooms. The Raven Suite. No one was supposed to be in there, and I knew I was the only person in that part of the building. I called out, but no one answered. The voices stopped as soon as I spoke. I almost dropped the linens and ran downstairs, but something stopped me. Shaking like a leaf, I went to the doorway to the suite.

"The door was open, which it shouldn't have been. And inside, I saw…." She paused, her eyes closed as if revisiting that night. "I saw a young man. Thin, with long blond hair. He was wearing jeans and no shirt. And he looked so lost. So sad. He was standing by the fireplace, and he just stared at me. And then he said something."

"What did he say?" I asked.

Mrs. Ramsey bit her lip. "He said, 'I can't find him. Help me find him.' It wasn't like a normal person talking, though. This was like the wind, words in the wind. It chilled me right to the bone. I let out a little cry and ran down the hall like a shot! How I got down the stairs without falling and breaking my neck I have no idea, but by the time I found Mr. Nelson I was a blubbering mess. He didn't believe me, of course. But some of the other staff did, and later we talked about our experiences."

"I've seen him too," I said. "Coleman Hollis."

She nodded. "Several of us tried to get the authorities to look into his disappearance. You can imagine how the police reacted when they found out we thought Coleman was dead because we'd seen his ghost. Anyway, we were told there was no evidence of foul play. So a few of us got a Ouija board and tried to contact Coleman's spirit."

"What happened?"

Mrs. Ramsey made a sour face. "The table we were using moved. Unfortunately, it turned out that it was just Billy Soames, shifting one of the legs with his feet. But me and a couple of others were serious about learning about Coleman and what happened to him. I looked into him and his family the two years I worked there, and tried and tried again to find out why he was haunting the Raven's Rest. I obsessed over it, really."

I gathered from the look on her face that the story didn't have a happy ending. "Did you learn anything?"

Shaking her head, Mrs. Ramsey said, "I never even saw the ghost again. Oh, I heard noises every now and then, or a door would open or close, but no spirit. Trey was just little then, starting school. And I guess I was spending too much time at the inn, even when I wasn't working. Walter, Trey's father, got fed up and left. And in the end, I learned nothing. Maybe there isn't anything to learn."

Mrs. Ramsey reached out and grabbed my hand, holding it in both of hers. "What I'm trying to say is, sometimes there's a mystery with no answer. I thought that if I could find out why Coleman's ghost was haunting the Raven's Rest... well, I thought I could help him. Get him to move on. Go on to heaven, if you will." She shook her head sadly. "But I couldn't. I don't think anyone can. And if you're seeing Coleman's ghost... well, I don't want you to make the same mistake I did."

"I'm not planning—"

She didn't let me finish. "I talked with Erin Hughes. She tells me you could have had a room at the Lincoln Apartments and moved in by now, but you held off putting in your application."

"I put in my application yesterday, actually. I just haven't figured out a date to move in." I had loads of reasons for delaying a move, but the reality was that I didn't want to leave the Raven's Rest until I knew what Coleman needed from me.

Mrs. Ramsey patted my hand. "You're a good person. I can tell. And I think you'll be good for Trey. God knows he needs someone good in his life. But as far as the Raven's Rest goes, my advice is to leave it be. Coleman Hollis will always reside within its walls. Whatever is keeping him there, nothing is going to change. So you don't fret about it. Just leave it be and get on with your life. Don't be talking to Jesenia Maupin and having her read her tarot cards for you. Just let it go."

I hadn't realized anyone knew about my chat with Jesenia, other than Trey, and I knew he hadn't said anything to his mother. "It just seems like he's calling out to me."

"I thought he was calling out to me too, all those years ago. But in the end, nothing happened. I found out zilch." She smiled encouragingly, then got to her feet. "Well, that's my say on the matter. Now maybe you'd better go check on Trey and make sure he hasn't broken every plate I own."

I nodded and went back to the kitchen. I appreciated Mrs. Ramsey's concern, of course, but I knew I had to keep trying to learn more about what happened to Coleman Hollis. After all, I had an advantage that she didn't have.

I was the spitting image of Coleman's lover, Bryan.

CHAPTER SEVEN

THE MOVIE had been the usual Hollywood drivel, but Trey and I enjoyed it, more for the company than anything happening on-screen. We had a huge bucket of popcorn, only half of which got eaten, and held hands during part of the movie like high school kids. As the credits rolled and we disengaged our hands so we could put our jackets back on, I did have a moment where I thought, *What the hell am I doing? I shouldn't fall for this guy. Sort out the mess that is your life first before dragging someone else into it.* But that thought was fleeting.

I liked Trey, and reason had absolutely no say in the matter.

As we walked back to his car, a beat-up Ford that suited him perfectly, Trey shuffled as he zipped up his coat and shivered. "Damn, it's getting cold."

"The little kids will have to wear coats over their costumes tomorrow night when they go trick-or-treating. I always hated that. Spider-Man never wore a coat over his tights."

"I should have known you went as Spider-Man." Trey's teeth were actually chattering as he fished out his keys.

"And I suppose you went as John Lennon or someone like that."

Trey smiled. "I did go as Tom Petty one year. No one knew who the hell I was supposed to be. Shows you what a dumb town this is."

"Good God, how old were you?" I asked as we got into the car. I immediately jammed my hands between my thighs to warm them. Trey was right. It was damned chilly.

"I was ten. I had Mom color my hair blond, and she glued fake sideburns onto my cheeks, and I wore this battered top hat and carried my electric guitar. People thought I was a rock-and-roll version of the Mad Hatter from *Alice in Wonderland*, which I guess is close. Pissed me off at the time, though." Trey started the engine and messed with the heating controls. Cold air poured out. "It'll warm up soon. So, home? Or there's this bar in town…."

"Let's go to the Raven's Rest. We can get some hot cocoa to warm ourselves up."

As it turned out, the kitchen was closed by the time we got there, so we had to forgo the drink. I did, however, invite Trey up to my room.

"Are you sure your ghost won't be jealous?" Trey said with a smirk.

"I'm hoping he's taking the night off." We were walking down the hallway, and I couldn't help but look at the door of the Raven Suite as we passed. If I could open the door, what would I find? An empty suite or a blast from the past? Would I see Coleman Hollis's room from 1984, complete with Boy George poster? I admit I rushed to get to my by-now-so-familiar Ulalume Suite.

Trey hovered by my side as I swiped the key card. "Kind of a disappointment, those things being used here. Ruins the old-world charm. They should have real keys."

"People lose real keys, and that can cost money. These are easier to replace, I think." I opened the door and stepped in. As I flicked the light switch, I tried to take in a sense of the room. In my days at the Raven's Rest, I'd learned to take note of the signs that told me I wasn't alone in the room: The hair on the back of my neck bristling. A sudden cold spot. The dimming of the lights.

The room seemed normal, and I breathed a sigh of relief. Trey followed me in, his mouth open as he took in the room. "You've been here how long? This must be setting you back a packet!"

"It's off-season, thankfully, so the rates are reduced. Still, it is gouging into my savings."

Trey slipped off his jacket and tossed it onto the bed as he gazed around. "Love the fireplace." He bounded over to the window and gazed out. "Nice view of the gazebo. Any ghosts hang out there?"

"None that I've seen, although Lonnie informs me apparitions are often spotted out there. Are you saying you're a believer now?"

Trey turned from the window and flashed me a wicked grin. "I'm still on the fence. When I see one, then I'll believe wholeheartedly."

I moved over to him, putting my arms around him. "They're pretty quiet tonight. Maybe they're gearing up for Halloween."

He kissed me briefly. I could still taste the popcorn butter on his lips. He stared into my eyes. "I wish I knew why I was so damned attracted to you." When he realized how that might be taken, he added, "You're so different from the guys I usually like."

"Funny. I was thinking the same thing about you."

"So what was your ex like? Kevin, I think you said his name was."

I pulled Trey close to me. "He was sexy as hell. He'd played basketball in high school, so he was the jock type. When we started going out, I thought he was Brad Pitt and Cary Grant and Peyton Manning all rolled into one."

"Interesting combination. Who's Cary Grant?"

"Actor back in the black-and-white days. The epitome of sophistication and charm, traits I soon learned that Kevin could only fake for short periods of time. He… well, let's just say he was moody. He yelled a lot. We fought constantly."

"So why did you stay with him so long?"

Because I thought I deserved him. Because he told me I couldn't live on my own. Aloud I said, "I'm not sure. I guess I always hoped he'd change. Become nicer." I really didn't want to talk about the past. The present was very much in my mind, and to get Trey thinking along the same lines, I put my hands on his butt and squeezed. "Do we really want to talk about Kevin?"

Trey smiled. "Who's Kevin?"

And then he kissed me. I was pretty sure I melted in his arms. We swayed a bit as I closed my eyes and put all thoughts but Trey out of my mind. His taste, his scent. The way he gently bit my tongue as we kissed. The way I could sense, through his lips and tongue and the way his muscles felt against me, that he was fighting back the urge to giggle when our swaying almost made us lose our footing and we collided against a chair. Even that couldn't make us break off that kiss.

When I opened my eyes, I found myself looking into his. There was a question there. My intuition was that he was wondering if we were going to go further, and if we were, if I was ready. To answer, I planted my lips against his with a fierce passion, and ground our pelvises together. If that didn't let my intentions be known, nothing would.

With a slight giggle, Trey forced me to back up until my legs came into contact with the bed. I began to peel off his black T-shirt. He scrambled to yank my sweater off me. Once we were both shirtless, we went back to kissing. My hands were all over him, on his neck, his back, and, briefly, on his firm buttocks. It was like I was desperate to touch every part of him. His skin felt warm and electric.

Trey pushed forward, and we both fell onto the bed, our lips parting for the briefest of moments as we bounced on the mattress. Trey was grinning like an ape. He was on top of me, and I have to say I liked feeling his weight on me. There was something secure about being able to look up into his face. I did notice that he had slight bags under his eyes, making me wonder if he'd been getting enough rest, and that he needed to trim his nose hairs. These imperfections, far from putting me off, made me like him even more. He was human. Not perfect by any means.

He slowly removed my glasses. "I don't think we'll be needing these," he said as he set them on the nightstand.

"Where did you go?" I said jokingly, patting the bedclothes at my sides theatrically, like I couldn't tell he was on top of me.

"Funny," Trey said.

We kissed again, and I fought the urge to just rip his jeans off him. His skin was so warm against mine, and he touched like he knew just where I liked to be touched. Trey raised himself off me slightly to run his fingers over my abdomen. Finally he gently groped my crotch. Again he looked at me questioningly, clearly wondering if he was going too far too fast.

I kicked off my sneakers. "Let's get comfortable," I said. Meaning naked.

Trey grinned and twisted off me. He was wearing black boots, so he had to unlace them before they'd come off. Once they were off, I saw he was sporting black socks as well. I should have known. He started to pull these off, but our lips hadn't been touching for what seemed ages, so I pulled him back on top of me, and we kissed. More groping ensued, and somehow I got his belt buckle undone and slipped my hand down inside his jeans. Getting past the elastic band of his underwear was difficult, but I was determined. Finally I brushed my fingers against his erection.

He pulled his lips off mine and gasped. Then he grinned mischievously. "I've been wanting to do this ever since you walked into the cafe that first day."

"Were you going to wait until we got somewhere private, or do me right there in front of the customers?"

"Right then, of course. You know how I like to shock people."

He'd undone my jeans and chose that moment to grasp my cock. Trey didn't go for a light, gentle touch either. He made damn sure I knew I'd been grabbed, and tightly. Cocky little bastard. I was too horny to notice a little pain, however.

"You just shocked me, I think." I whispered the words.

He squeezed harder, his eyes gleaming. "Good. I like to know I've got your attention."

We were now pretty much side by side to allow access to each other's genitals. Trey released his grip on my dick and cupped my face in his hands. Much as I liked feeling his hands on my erection, I decided he could touch me anywhere and it would send delicious shivers down my spine. He kissed me gently.

"I really like you, Michael," he said.

"And I—"

The lightbulb in the lamp on the nightstand exploded.

"What the—" Trey exclaimed as the bulb in the overhead fixture shattered as well, with a loud popping sound. The lamp on the desk went too, plunging us into darkness. Trey rolled off me, and I could see the shock in his face, as there was just enough moonlight coming in through the window.

"My God," I whispered.

Maybe I had been too immersed in my own lust to notice that there'd been a change in the room. Now, though, I could feel the cold and that sense that we weren't alone. I sat up, reaching out for Trey's hand. He grasped it hard, and I could see him looking around the room, waiting for whatever came next.

"Ah, shit!" he yelled, pulling his hand free and putting it up to his cheek.

"What is it?" I demanded.

"Something fucking scratched me!"

I tried to grab Trey's face to turn it toward the window so I could see if, indeed, he'd been scratched, but he was too freaked out and batted my hands away. And then I looked over Trey's shoulder and saw a misty figure standing by the bed.

It was Coleman Hollis. He wasn't solid, and there was no color to him. Just a pale figure. I couldn't even see his legs. Below his waist, there was just mist. But all I needed to see was his face, which was set in a look of pure hatred. Coleman's face was twisted, and his eyes blazed with malice.

Trey was obviously unaware of the figure, and he turned toward me. "I think I'm bleeding," he said, staring at the darkened stains on his fingers.

I put an arm around Trey's shoulders and gazed into the apparition's angry face. "I'm not Bryan," I said through gritted teeth. "Please stop doing this!"

The face lost none of its animosity, but as I held Trey close to me, the figure slowly vanished. I waited until there was no sign left, no mist, no feeling of someone unseen in the room, and then I got to my feet, put my glasses back on, and pulled Trey, who was holding his cheek and cussing under his breath, into the bathroom. The light there had escaped the bulb shattering, and we both blinked when I flicked on the switch.

Trey's face had three welts running along his left cheek, one gouge deep enough that it had broken the skin. I helped him over to the sink and turned on the faucets. "Let's wash you up."

Trey was in shock. He didn't seem to understand my words and made no move to clean off the blood, so I snagged a washcloth off the rack and got it nice and wet. Trey turned toward me only when I moved him, and it wasn't until I touched his cheek with the cloth that any life showed in his eyes.

"What the fuck just happened?" he asked in a small voice.

I didn't answer that. Instead I said, "It doesn't look deep. I don't think you'll have a scar." My smile was meant to reassure him. I don't think it did.

I daubed at his cheek, causing the white cloth to become pink as it soaked up Trey's blood. He was pale, but at least now his eyes showed animation. "I just got scratched by a fucking ghost, didn't I?"

"Yeah, I'm afraid so," I replied. I hated the look of fear in Trey's eyes. There was no way I was going to tell him about the figure I'd seen. Maybe later, once he'd recovered more.

He sighed and stared into my eyes. "I think I'm falling in love with you, Michael. But, and I mean this, I'm never setting foot in this room again. And I don't want you to either. Let's get the fuck out of here."

I nodded, and we went out and grabbed our clothes. I think Trey broke records getting his gear back on, even though his fingers shook as he attempted to lace his boots. We dressed by the light coming in from the bathroom. There was no way I was going to chance turning on other lamps in the bedroom, afraid the bulbs might meet the same fate as the ones that had shattered. Once we were ready, we grabbed our jackets and headed for the door. Automatically I reached for the light switch, but there was no light to turn off. I closed the door firmly behind us.

"I need a drink," Trey said as he walked rapidly down the hall.

I looked back at the door, falling a few paces behind Trey. Even though I'd made it seem like I agreed with him about not returning to the Ulalume Suite, I knew I would.

My business there was unfinished.

CHAPTER EIGHT

I HELPED Trey in the front door of the big old farmhouse where he lived with his mother and God knows how many cousins and aunts. He was doing better, but he still had a slightly distracted air about him as he stumbled along. If I hadn't been there to guide him up the porch steps, he'd have fallen face-first, causing more damage. I could tell he was still trying to make sense out of what had occurred. Good luck there.

His mom was watching television in the living room, but as soon as she caught sight of the scratches she was up out of her chair, fussing over him and asking questions neither of us knew how to answer. She forced him onto a small bench in the foyer so she could get a better look at his cheek.

"How did this happen?" she demanded of me, as she was getting only noncommittal replies from Trey.

"I don't—"

Luckily, Trey's Aunt Janet (another Coffee Cafe employee), emerged from a back room at that moment, drawn by Mrs. Ramsey's raised voice. The two of them took turns turning Trey's face this way and that, getting the best view. "What in the world have you been doing?" Janet asked him.

"Pissing off a ghost, it seems," Trey answered with a weak smile.

Trey's mother and aunt immediately stopped their fussing and stood up straight, their voices now silent. Janet crossed herself.

Mrs. Ramsey started to speak, realized she had no words, and closed her mouth. She repeated this process again before finally finding words. "What the hell are you talking about?"

Trey told them what had happened, leaving out the fact that we were in the process of fondling each other and getting naked when the lightbulb erupted. Some details just weren't necessary. He finished by saying, "Needless to say, we hightailed it out of there, and I'm never setting foot in that place again."

"Well, I should hope not!" His mother was nearly shouting. She turned to me. "And neither are you. You're staying here until you get your apartment. I'll make up the couch in the family room, and you can sleep there."

"He can stay in my room," Trey protested.

Gloria seemed about to argue but apparently decided it was a lost cause. "Okay, but I don't want to hear you boys bumping and grinding all night. You know how thin these walls are."

I felt I should point out some things. "My stuff is still at the Raven's Rest."

"Trey has clothes you can wear for now." Never mind that they'd be tight on me and that my legs were longer than his.

Shaking my head, I said, "I'll be fine at the inn. Really."

Janet looked at me like I'd just sprouted an extra head. "Are you crazy? Weren't you there when this happened? When Trey got scratched?"

"Yes, but…." I didn't really know how to finish that sentence. I sighed. "I have to go back."

"There's no 'have to' about it," Gloria said. "You're staying here."

"I'll be safe." I tried my reassuring smile on them, although I was sure it came out weak. "It's Coleman's ghost. Coleman Hollis. He won't hurt me." When I saw a question forming on Gloria's lips, I added, "I resemble Coleman's boyfriend."

Trey's mother let this sink in a moment before saying, "Well, that may be worse! What if he… you know… tries to mess with you."

The thought of being groped by a ghost hadn't actually occurred to me. "I don't think that will happen."

"And I'm sure Trey thought he wouldn't get mauled either!"

"Mom, I wasn't—"

"Hush, you! I'm trying to knock some sense into your boyfriend!"

"We're not—" Trey was blushing.

Gloria rolled her eyes heavenward. "If you aren't yet, you will be. Don't think we haven't noticed you two making cow eyes at each other all week."

Trey looked to his aunt for support, but Janet merely smiled. "We all know. If fact, we've all been wondering why you two are taking so long."

I smiled at that, as I'd felt like Trey and I were going too fast as it was. A different perspective, I guessed. "I'll be okay," I repeated.

Trey glared at me. "You're an idiot if you go back there."

"I need to."

He blinked. "I still like you, even if I do think you're being stupid."

"Thanks, I think."

The discussion was curtailed while Gloria went to get some disinfectant for Trey's wound. She and Janet took turns daubing the scratches with a Q-tip dipped in alcohol. Trey hissed several times, either from the burning of the medicine or from the women poking him with the Q-tips. They decided a bandage wasn't necessary, nor was it practical since the scratches were so long.

"We could cover the whole cheek with gauze," Janet suggested.

Trey was dubious. "I think I'll be fine. I'll live."

Once it was clear that Trey was over the shock of our experience and was back to his usual self, I began to inch closer to the front door. "I really should be going now."

"Don't," Trey said.

"He's right," Gloria added. "At least stay tonight."

I shook my head. "I know this doesn't make any sense, but I feel like I need to be there tonight."

Gloria frowned. "There are no answers to be found there. I told you that before."

"I know. Still, I have to try."

Trey started to stand up, saying, "Crap! I drove! You can't walk back to the inn. I'll drive you."

"I can walk, thanks. You stay and rest."

Gloria took both my hands in hers and held them tightly. "I wish I could convince you to stay."

"I'll be fine. It's only a few blocks." Actually, it was close to six, but still easily within walking distance.

"You be careful." There was worry in her eyes.

"I will."

Gloria scored points with me by realizing that Trey and I might want to be alone to say good night and invented a crisis in the kitchen that needed both her and Janet's attention. When they'd gone, Trey stood, still a little shaky, and put his arms around me.

"How did you get to be so stubborn?" he asked.

"I'm not sure. I think I'm getting strength from you. God knows I haven't had any on my own these last few years."

Trey thought about that. "No, I think it's the inn. Now you've found a purpose. Some puzzle that you've got to solve." He grinned. "And me, of course. Some of my tough has worn off on you."

"Yeah, you're a whole a hundred and forty pounds of tough."

"One forty-five, I'll have you know."

"Oooh. Such a stud." Our embrace became tighter.

"More stud than you'll ever need."

I hoped so. We kissed, a long, lingering one, and reluctantly I opened the door and walked out into the chilly night.

I hadn't gone far before I began to regret not taking Trey up on his offer of a ride. For one thing, it was getting colder, and my hands were quickly chilled. I'd left my gloves on the dresser back at the Raven's Rest, so I jammed my fists into my jacket pockets and increased my steps. My shoes scuffed reassuringly on the cement sidewalk.

But there was another sound, somewhere behind me. A shuffling. Like someone was trailing me.

I stopped and turned but could see no one. Deciding it was just my imagination, I went on.

My own muffled footsteps, that distinct sound of rubber soles on cement, were being echoed. I was sure of it. I stopped again. This time the sounds behind me continued for a second. As I turned, I could have sworn I saw a shadow dart behind one of the trees lining the avenue, a half block behind me.

"Who's there?" I called out. "Trey?"

That was an act of the purest optimism, yelling out his name. I knew he hadn't followed me. He certainly wouldn't act surreptitious if he had. So who was it? A mugger? In Banning? Did Banning *have* muggers?

There was no further movement over by the tree, and I began to wonder if I had been mistaken. The moon was out and bright, throwing shadows everywhere. Maybe I'd just seen the shadow of a tree branch or something. After the evening I'd had, I was understandably jumpy and liable to assume the worst.

Slowly, I continued on my way, straining my ears for any unusual sound. Somewhere nearby, an owl was hooting. I could hear a car or two, likely on the more traveled roads closer to Washington Street, blocks away from where I was. Other than that, the night was quiet.

Behind me, a twig snapped, and I twisted around to see a dark figure darting behind the cover of a bush. It was impossible in the light provided to get much detail, but I could tell the person was tall and thin and seemed to be wearing a dark jacket and a hat of some kind.

A brave person might have strode purposely up to the bush and demanded that the person show himself. Me, I turned and ran.

It wasn't even a conscious decision. I think my legs decided for me. I didn't even know if my stalker followed me. All I knew was that I was bolting down the sidewalk, praying that someone would come out of their house to see what the commotion was about. Then I could have them call the police. I had my cell phone on me, but I immediately dismissed the thought of pausing to fish it out of my pocket. In my mind, by the time I slowed down and got my mitts on it, my pursuer would catch up with me and slit my throat, or whatever he planned on doing to me.

I ran two blocks, gasping and puffing, before daring to slow down enough to glance behind me. Nothing. No movement anywhere. Not even a stray cat. I felt like collapsing from relief, and just then a car turned the corner ahead of me and I could see, from the illumination provided by a streetlight, that it had *Sheriff's Department* emblazoned on the side. I waved my arms frantically.

The car stopped, and I found myself suddenly blinded by the searchlight attached to the driver's side of the car. I heard a voice I recognized asking, "Can I help you, sir?"

It was Erin Hughes, the deputy I'd met at the Raven's Rest. Out of breath, I gasped, "There's someone… following me. Or was. I think they're gone now."

The light was extinguished, and Deputy Hughes stepped out of the vehicle. "Mr. Cook, isn't it?"

"Yes." I could finally get my words out without wheezing. "I was walking back from the Ramseys' house, and I heard someone following me."

Deputy Hughes joined me on the sidewalk, and she flicked on a powerful flashlight, scanning the area. "Did you see them?" she asked.

I was thankful she didn't sound dismissive. In Rockford, I was sure a cop would have almost laughed at a young man complaining of being followed. "Yeah. Once when I turned around, I saw someone darting behind a bush. Back there. A block or two back." I waved in the direction I'd come.

"What did they look like? Did you see their face?" Hughes was still shining her light around, even though I could tell by her face that she thought it unlikely she'd see anything.

"It was too dark. All I could tell was they were tall. And thin. And I think they were wearing a duffle-type coat. You know the type I mean?"

The blonde woman nodded. "I'd say you shook them off, whoever it was. Probably just one of the local kids, trying to scare a stranger as a Halloween prank. Unless you know of anyone who might have been…." She let the statement dangle.

I shook my head. "No, I can't think of anyone who would." The idea of it being just a neighborhood kid didn't seem right either. While I couldn't put my finger on why, I'd felt a definite threat from the figure's presence, more than would come from some rowdy teenager out to scare a stranger. I couldn't explain that sensation to Deputy Hughes, though. I had nothing to back up my notion.

She turned off her flashlight. "I'm betting it was Doug West. One of our less productive dropouts. He's always roaming the streets at night, and this is just the sort of thing he'd think was hilarious."

"You're probably right," I said, not believing it for a minute.

"Want me to give you a lift back to the Raven's Rest?"

I took a deep breath while pondering. I could see the inn, just a block and a half away. "No, I think I'm fine."

"I'll drive around, see if I can find anyone lurking about. You call us if you have any further problems, Mr. Cook."

"I will. I can promise you that." My heart had only just stopped threatening to burst through my chest. I gave the deputy a salute of farewell and resumed my trek to my room.

"Why," I muttered to myself as soon as I was out of earshot of Hughes, "didn't you take Trey up on his offer to stay with him? You could be in his arms right now, rather than shaking from fear."

Erin Hughes got back into her car, and moments later she sped off down the road. I doubted she'd find a trace of my stalker. I knew, though, it wasn't any teenager. No, someone had been following me, and their intent had been malicious.

But who had it been? And why?

CHAPTER NINE

"THIS IS it," Trey said.

I didn't know what I had been expecting, but it certainly wasn't a little white cottage surrounded by a picket fence. Somehow I'd expected Jesenia Maupin to live in something more esoteric, strange. Not a fairy-tale witch's hovel, but at least something with some history to it, like a mock Tudor home or a Victorian folly. The place Trey indicated was just so… average.

Maybe when you rang the doorbell, the theme from *The Addams Family* rang through the tiny house. That would suit the woman and her vibe.

I opened the gate and held it for Trey. "After you," I said.

"Oh no. This is your idea. You lead the way."

As we went up the short walk, it occurred to me that Jesenia hadn't even decorated for Halloween. No orange lights, no ghosts hanging from the branches of her trees. There wasn't even a pumpkin to greet us on the porch.

"You sure you want to do this?" Trey asked.

I was. When I had returned to my room at the Raven's Rest after my ordeal of being followed, I'd found nothing waiting for me. The room had been eerily quiet. More than that, though, I had the distinct feeling that I was being snubbed, that the spirit was pissed at me and was refusing to come around.

Probably I was reading too much into the situation. Didn't they say that ghosts required energy to manifest themselves? And it must have taken a hell of a lot of energy to shatter light bulbs and rake ghostly fingernails across Trey's cheek. Surely the spirit of Coleman Hollis was just out of power and was recuperating. Still, I couldn't shake the feeling that I had, in some way, disappointed the spirit.

I needed to talk to him. Soon. Find out what he wanted. And my best bet for doing that was Jesenia Maupin.

She answered the door wearing a bright blue tunic and black slacks. Her button wasn't affixed to her breast, which I found oddly disappointing. As she held the door open for us, she said, "I've been expecting you."

She took us to a room she called her parlor, which was quaint and decorated with loads of little knickknacks everywhere, most of which were frogs. "I like frogs," she explained when she saw Trey gaping at her collection. "Sit. What can I do for you boys?"

Trey perched himself on the edge of an uncomfortable-looking settee. I sat on a wicker chair that creaked under my weight but held me. I glanced at Trey for support, but he was staring at a huge green ceramic frog that was eyeing him from the coffee table. Sighing, I asked Jesenia, "Can you do a séance?"

"Of course I can 'do a séance.'" She mimicked my phrasing. "The question is, should I do one?"

"I think so. Coleman Hollis is trying to tell me something. He's tried to tell people before, and he's never succeeded. There's something he wants us to know, and we just aren't listening. Not in the right ways, I guess."

Jesenia scooped up a cat that had been snoozing on a pillow on her sofa. The animal barely woke up and seemed untroubled by the disturbance. Sitting, Jesenia placed the cat on her lap, and the feline immediately resumed its slumber. She stroked the cat's back and said, "Are you prepared for the consequences?"

"Consequences?"

"It's always been assumed that Coleman Hollis ran off, that he left town all those years ago. If you prove that his spirit haunts the Raven's Rest... well, people in town still remember him. His father still lives here. You'll be dredging up a nasty can of worms."

"Wouldn't his father want to know what happened? I think it would provide some closure."

Jesenia nodded. "I agree. Always best to know. I just wanted you to know that there may be repercussions." The cat shifted positions so Jesenia could rub its tummy. "But I feel that, to be truly effective, the séance should be held at the Raven's Rest. Preferably in your room, since that's where the manifestations seem to be concentrated." She glanced at Trey's cheek, still red and sore-looking. "Did you get that at the inn?"

Trey touched the wound. "Yeah. I think we made old Cole a little jealous."

"I think you should be there."

"I… I really don't think so." Trey's eyes were wide. "He doesn't like me. That's obvious. Let's not give him the chance to gouge the other cheek or do something worse."

Jesenia frowned. "He's confused. From what you told me on the phone, Michael here resembles his lover. This will be a good opportunity to straighten things out. Let him know that you're no threat."

"I'd say he's the one doing the threatening." I could see Trey was relenting a little, though. Finally he sighed. "I'll be there. Dammit, tonight's Halloween. I'd planned on just sitting at home—hopefully cuddling with a certain someone—and watching *The Wolf Man*."

"We'll start the séance at midnight," Jesenia said cheerily. "That'll give you time to get your movie in. It's short, if I remember correctly." She clapped her hands and grinned at us. "So! Midnight it is, then!"

The cat raised its head and looked disgruntled about the noise she was making.

TRICK-OR-TREATING WAS, according to the newspaper, to be held between four and seven o'clock, after which there was a "costume parade" and party at the town's community center. It wasn't quite four, but already some little ghosts and goblins and superheroes were trickling into the Raven's Rest on their rounds to collect candy. Lonnie Schultz, dressed as a devil (complete with red cape), was manning the desk, and he had a huge bowl of candy waiting for them.

"Wow. That's a really good Batman. And who are you? A princess? You're so pretty, Your Majesty! Here you go!"

The kids, giggling, ran out of the inn, on to their next stop. Lonnie couldn't wipe the grin off his face. He was obviously enjoying his role of candy distributor.

"Hey, Mr. Cook—"

"Michael."

"Mike. How are things? Still staying through the weekend?"

"I plan on it. Maybe longer. I have yet to buy furniture, and I really don't want to start living in a totally empty apartment. How's business?"

"Good. Especially for this time of year. We have several new people checked in, so if you see someone new in the halls, it's probably a real person, not a ghost." He laughed at his own joke.

"Is there someone in the Raven Suite? I heard noises coming from there this morning as I walked past."

"Yeah, a guy who checked in last night. I hope he didn't disturb you. But hey, after the lightbulb incident, I'm guessing not much really disturbs you."

I had, of course, confided in Lonnie first thing when I'd come downstairs in the morning. Well, someone had to replace the bulbs, and I didn't want the staff to think I was some weird guy who went around destroying lighting sources. Lonnie, who seemed to never be off work, had personally come up with fresh bulbs, his mouth hanging open in awe as he examined the damaged lamps.

"No, he didn't bother me at all. I just wondered," I said. I'd known, somehow, that the sounds coming from the Raven Suite were from a living, breathing human. They hadn't raised goose bumps or made the hairs on the back of my neck bristle. "About the lightbulbs…."

"Oh, hey. No worries. These things happen." Lonnie frowned. "Well, actually, nothing like *that* has happened before. We've had guests see things, been touched, felt suddenly cold, but exploding lights is a new one."

"I know I told you not to tell anyone about it…."

"And I didn't! It's just between you and me, Mr. Cook!"

"The thing is," I said, with what I hoped was an ingratiating smile, "I really believe Coleman Hollis is trying to tell me something. I just can't figure out what it is. So I've enlisted the aid of Jesenia Maupin—"

"The witch?"

Lonnie looked immediately sorry that he'd blurted out the words, so I merely carried on. "And I want her to conduct a séance. In my room here."

Lonnie took a deep breath. "A séance? That's… heavy stuff."

"How do you think your mother will react? I could just sneak Jesenia up to my room, but I feel like I should tell your mom what we're doing. After all, it's her place."

With a sheepish grin, Lonnie leaned over the counter to speak to me in a conspiratorial manner. "Actually, Mr. Cook, I did tell her about the lightbulb thing. Well, you see, she was talking this afternoon about how—"

We were interrupted as another group of trick-or-treaters arrived. The mother hung back while a tiny witch, a skeleton, and a vaguely disturbing Wonder Woman (did a five-year-old really need to be wearing boots with high heels?) grabbed some candy for their pumpkins. Satisfied, they quickly exited and Lonnie went on.

"Anyway, she was saying how we hadn't had anything spooky happen for some time now, and I told her how wrong she was. You know, sort of rubbing her face in it. I didn't mention you by name, just said it happened in one of the rooms, but she figured out who it was. Well, we really don't have too many people staying here right now, and she knew it wouldn't be the Clark family, because they've got little kids, and—"

"It's okay, Lonnie. I don't mind that you told her. It'll make it easier to talk to her about my proposal. Do you know where she is right now?"

Lonnie rubbed his chin. "She'll be in the dining room, most likely. I don't know if she's going to be so hot on the idea of a séance, though. She doesn't want to scare people away from staying here, you know."

"No one need know about it other than just us. I'll see what she says. I'm sure I can convince her."

The truth was, I really hadn't talked much with Lonnie's mother. She'd manned the front desk only a few times during my stay, and other than saying hi and bye, we'd hardly exchanged words. In a way I found her slightly intimidating. She always seemed friendly enough, but she didn't possess Lonnie's exuberant nature. A big woman, it always seemed like the smile could easily leave her face and you'd be left with a woman you really didn't want to mess with.

And I was about to spring one hell of a suggestion on her.

Betty Schultz was, indeed, in the dining room, chatting with one of her workers. When I entered, her serious expression was replaced with a welcoming grin, although I did see her steal a glance at the wall clock.

"Mr. Cook! How nice to see you! It's a little early for dinner, but I'm sure we can—"

"Actually, I just wanted to have a word with you, if I may."

The employee was dismissed, and Mrs. Schultz gave me her undivided attention. "I guess you've heard about the lightbulb thing—"

I didn't actually get the last word entirely out before Mrs. Schultz held up her hands. "Mr. Cook, I can assure you that the whole thing can be easily explained. I know it's easy to go right to the ghost explanation, but a sudden power surge can cause quite a lot of havoc. Naturally, if you want to move to another room—"

Power surge. How stupid did she think I was? Still, I'm sure she was only trying to put a positive spin on the event. "Actually," I said, "I want to hold a séance. With your permission."

She froze. "A séance?"

"You know, sitting around a table, holding hands. 'Anyone out there want to talk to anyone in here.' That sort of thing."

A frown furrowed her brow. "I know what a séance is, Mr. Cook. I've seen the movies. I just don't think we need one."

"I respectfully disagree. Coleman Hollis is trying to tell us something, and I want to know what it is. I think the best way to communicate with him is through a séance. Jesenia Maupin can act as the medium. I—"

"Jesenia Maupin!"

Why did everyone act like she was a laughable lunatic? Well, other than the fact that Jesenia presented herself as a laughable lunatic....

It took a good ten minutes, but I finally persuaded Betty Schultz to agree to a séance. I had to go through every ghostly incident that had happened to me in detail, and even threw in what I'd heard from

Gloria Ramsey, but eventually Lonnie's mother relented. She did, however, have several stipulations.

"I don't want this to get around. Certainly not into the newspapers."

"No problem."

"And I want to be there."

That made me blink. "Sure. Of course." I figured she wanted to make sure things didn't get out of hand, but then she explained.

"I've always loved the history of this house. It's part of the reason I bought the place. So if there's a chance I'll get to talk to someone who lived here in the past, before it was turned into an inn, I want to be there."

I nodded. "Jesenia thinks midnight would be a good time."

"I'll be there, Mr. Cook."

CHAPTER TEN

"I'M CREEPED out, and we haven't even started yet," Trey said.

"Can't imagine why," I muttered, loud enough for him to hear. We were in the Ulalume Suite with Jesenia, waiting for Betty Schultz to join us. She promised that, although she had some business to attend to, she'd make it well before the clock struck midnight.

"There's nothing to worry about," Jesenia assured Trey. "The spirits in this place have retreated. I think they're a little nervous around me. They haven't quite figured me out yet. Once I've reassured them, we'll get some answers."

There was a brisk knock at the door, and I let Mrs. Schultz in. For once, her forbidding countenance was replaced with a trace of nervousness. As she walked in, she gazed about the room.

"I was half expecting to find the furniture all upside down and covered with ectoplasm, or whatever they call that shit. You know, *Ghostbusters* slime."

"Ectoplasm is real, but it isn't green like it was in the film." Jesenia was busy getting the little round table set up, placing four chairs around it. She'd already placed a candle in a stick in the center. "Michael dear, would you close those curtains? I'm afraid the moon is a bit too bright tonight."

Trey was closer, and he seemed to need something to do, so he adjusted the blinds and drapes. "Are we going to see a ghost?" he asked.

"Hopefully, darling." Obviously satisfied with the table, Jesenia looked around the room critically. "The fire is okay, but can you adjust it a little, Michael? A little less flame?"

I got the gas flame to her liking, and Jesenia nodded. "I think we're ready now. Betty, I'm really glad you're joining us. I haven't seen you since the Petunia Festival."

Mrs. Schultz didn't seem inclined to reminisce. "How long is this going to take? I have to get up early and help see to breakfast."

Jesenia sat and did a one-shoulder shrug. "It takes as long as it takes. Since Michael already seems to have an affinity with the spirits here, I'd wager that things could heat up rather quickly, but I'm not making any promises. Trey darling, would you get the lights? And would everyone be seated."

Mrs. Schultz started to sit down opposite Jesenia, but Trey quickly moved from the light switch and ushered her into the chair on Jesenia's left. I think he wanted to make sure we'd be sitting next to each other. That was okay with me. I assumed we'd be holding hands or at least touching them together like they did in the movies, and I could use his support. My heart was beating fast, and I was already finding it hard to breathe, and so far the scariest thing the evening had provided had been a ten-year-old trick-or-treating as the alien from *Predator*. Anticipating something frightening could almost be worse than the frightening thing itself.

Jesenia placed her hands flat on the table. "Please make sure that your fingers are touching the person's next to you. The circle must not be broken once we've established contact."

"Shit," Trey muttered. "I've got to pee."

"This isn't a time for jest," Jesenia warned him with a frown.

"No, I'm serious. I've got to pee."

We paused while Trey went to the bathroom to relieve himself. Once he'd resumed his seat, I smiled at him. "Told you to go before we started."

"Shut up."

Once everyone was back in position, Jesenia closed her eyes. Her face looked odd, lit only by the candle and the little flame she'd allowed in the fireplace. Serene, but eerily pale and unnatural, as if she were made of wax. "We wish to communicate with the spirits who live within the walls of the Raven's Rest. We wish to speak with Coleman Hollis. Coleman, are you there?"

Nothing happened, and I heard Trey breathe a sigh of relief.

"You mustn't be afraid. We're not here to hurt you. We make no demands of you. We only wish to talk with you."

The candle flame guttered slightly, but that might have been from a draft. I didn't know how a closed room with no air-conditioning or heating on could have a draft, but I preferred that explanation. My uneasiness amused me a little. I wanted to learn what Coleman had to say, but the séance was making me jumpy, and the butterflies in my stomach were giving me the willies. It was like getting on a roller coaster. You wanted the thrill, but that didn't stop you from wondering, just as you got at the top of the hill, if you hadn't make a horrible mistake in judgment.

"Coleman," Jesenia went on, "Michael here has felt your presence. He's heard you speak before. Speak to us now, Coleman. Tell us why you're not at rest!"

"Oh." Betty Schultz visibly shivered. "I just felt something cold. A breeze against my back. Like someone just opened a refrigerator."

"I felt it too," Trey said.

I hadn't, and that was odd, as Trey was opposite Mrs. Schultz. Maybe whatever it was had gone *through* the table, rather than around it. I did, however, feel a change in the room's atmosphere. I was certain the four of us weren't the only presences in the room.

"Someone is here," Jesenia intoned. "Coleman, is that you?"

The candle guttered again, and this time I knew it was no natural breeze causing the flickering. Part of me wanted to jump up out of my chair and run, being a chicken at heart. Knowing I'd never hear the end of it from Trey kept me rooted to the spot. Besides, this was what I wanted. Answers. I just wish they didn't come cloaked in the macabre.

And then I heard it. A voice, a mere whisper.

"Bryan."

My gaze darted over to Trey, and I could tell he'd heard it as well. His mouth was hanging open, and his eyes showed fear and awe, mostly awe. I could almost hear him thinking, *No way!* Or was I just projecting my thoughts onto him?

"Coleman, we know that you're here with us." Jesenia opened her eyes slowly. "Please speak to us. Tell us what you want."

"Bryan."

"He thinks I'm his boyfriend, Bryan," I said softly, not wanting to disrupt the proceedings.

Jesenia nodded, just a slight inclination of the head. "Coleman, this is Michael here with us. Michael Cook. I know you're confused, because he looks like someone you knew, someone you loved. Do you have a message for Michael?"

"*Not... Bryan....*"

The words were pained and anguished, and it hurt my heart to hear them. I was about to say something, some words to try to ease Coleman's sorrow if I could, when Betty Schultz muttered, "Oh my God."

I followed her gaze, as did Trey. Standing behind Jesenia was a figure. At first it was just a shadow, but slowly details began to emerge. Blond hair, prominent nose, melancholy eyes. Coleman Hollis. He appeared to be solid, although the colors were still muted, like he was bathed in moonlight. There was a sad smile on his face, and he was gazing directly at me.

"Holy...," Trey whispered.

Jesenia didn't move, but she realized there was something behind her by our reactions.

"Coleman, are you there?"

"He's there, all right," Mrs. Schultz said in a weak voice. "I can see him."

"Coleman, speak to Michael. He knows there's a message you want to impart."

The figure didn't speak, but his face was full of remorse, and he appeared to be crying.

I swallowed hard, then licked my lips. My vocal cords didn't want to work at first, but I forced some words out. "Coleman, I'm not Bryan. I know you loved him. I'd like to help you, if I can."

"*Where is he? Where is Bryan?*"

"I don't know. Maybe I can help you find him."

Trey muttered, "Holy shit." He couldn't take his eyes off the figure. None of us could, save Jesenia, who was watching my face.

"*Where's Bryan?*"

I realized the words were there, but Coleman's lips never moved. I wondered if the others could hear him, or if the words were only in my head. Trey answered my question by saying, "Oh my God, he sounds so sad."

"We want to help you, Coleman," I said. "Tell us what you need."

The spirit's face went from distressed to angry. His lips curled, and he let out a loud roar, full of inconsolable grief. As he did, the table jumped beneath our hands, just a little at first, but then it shot up several inches off the floor. All of us jumped back in shock. Mrs. Schultz put her fingers to her lips to try to keep from crying out as the candlestick overturned, the wick extinguished.

Everything seemed to happen at once. The table dropped back down with a crash, and the candlestick rolled off, clattering to the floor. The tiny gas fire suddenly erupted into a blaze, and I could hear the scrape of furniture on the floor. Out of the corner of my eye, I realized it was the writing desk, shooting several feet in our direction. The curtains billowed—even though I could see the window was shut tight—and the blinds crashed to the ground. Betty Schultz screamed, and Trey shouted something. Jesenia, a worried look on her face, was saying something to Coleman, who had now vanished, trying to calm him. The books on the shelf—a Bible, a dictionary, and a volume of inspirational quotes—went flying across the room. I had left my keys and money clip and a few other things on top of the entertainment center, and these scattered, as if brushed away by an invisible hand. The door to the bathroom slammed shut with enough force to shake the walls.

My chair suddenly shifted under my weight, and I felt it falling backward. I flailed, trying to keep it from falling—and me with it—but it overturned, and the wind was knocked out of me as I hit the floor. I lay there awkwardly, my legs tangled with those of the chair, and tried to catch my breath.

Then the room dimmed once more as the fire in the fireplace went back to the level we'd set it at, and everything was quiet, save for Mrs. Schultz's weeping.

Jesenia stood and put a hand on her chest, as if trying to quiet her heartbeat. "Trey," she said softly, "would you get the lights, please."

He ignored her, coming to my side instead. He helped me up, asking, "Are you okay?"

"I think so. Sort of."

"Oh my God," Mrs. Schultz whimpered. "I had no idea. I didn't think… I had no idea it would… I didn't think this would happen."

Jesenia seemed barely ruffled, compared to the rest of us, although even her voice was strained. "You never know what's going to happen once you begin a séance. Opening the veil like that, well, it can be tricky." She put a hand on Mrs. Schultz's shoulder. "Are you going to be all right, Betty?"

Mrs. Schultz sniffed and wiped her eyes. "I'm fine. I think. Just shocked, I guess. I thought we might hear a knock or two, maybe feel a cold spot. I never dreamed I'd see...."

Once he was sure I hadn't broken anything, Trey went over and switched on the lights. We all blinked as we surveyed the damage. The table was scratched where the candlestick had fallen, like it had been savagely drawn across the woodwork. The books were lying, one of them open, a good five feet away from the shelf. My coins and keys were all over the place. The blinds were in a heap at the window's base.

"Well, that was interesting," Jesenia said to no one in particular.

Trey returned and put an arm around me. He was shaking. Or maybe I was. It was hard to tell.

"Interesting?" Mrs. Schultz laughed hollowly. "That's an understatement."

"I think I have to pee again," Trey said, forcing a chuckle.

My heart was beating fast, and I was breathing as if I'd just run a mile. There was sweat on my brow despite the chill in the room. One arm was around Trey, but I kept the other on my chest, just in case the old ticker tried to give up and just stop. "I know one thing," I said.

"What's that?"

I looked at Trey. "I'm staying at your place tonight."

CHAPTER ELEVEN

I OPENED my eyes in the morning and saw Trey lying next to me, his face beautiful in repose. Sleeping soundly, he resembled a cherub from some old tapestry—angelic face untroubled by care. Okay, few cherubs were depicted as having long black locks and, yes, still visible scratch marks on his cheek—red welts that were, thankfully, looking less painful. To me, though, he was beauty itself.

As I watched him, Trey opened one eye. "Okay," he mumbled, still groggy from sleep, "you're watching me sleep. That's fucking creepy."

I smiled. "Sorry. Won't do it again."

"No, feel free. I like creepy. I've embraced the creepy in my life. Bring on the creepy. Mind you, no more séances. Not for, oh, say, another fifty years or so. By then it won't be so surprising when I wee in my pants."

"You didn't—"

"Felt like it, though." He propped himself up on one elbow and stroked my cheek. "You were fantastic last night."

"I was about to say the same about you."

He leaned in until our lips touched. His breath was slightly sour, but I didn't care.

"Wanna do it again?" he whispered.

I flicked the covers down so we could have better access to each other. We were both naked and hard. As we kissed our bodies melded together. "What do you think?"

"I think," he said, our lips brushing as he spoke, "that you're going to be pretty good for me, Michael Cook."

I touched his cheek gently. "Even though things like this happen when I'm around?"

His smile was wicked. "A little scratch won't keep me away from you."

"Oh, yeah. I forgot. You're a tough guy."

Eyes sparkling, he forced me onto my back. Slipping on top of me, he kissed me hard, one hand on my neck and the other slowly moving down my side. "You bet your ass I am."

"You keep saying you are, but so far all I've seen is Trey the pussycat."

"Oh? You wanna see Trey the tiger? You ready for that?" he laughed.

"I'm more than ready."

Trey slammed his weight against me, making me wince just a little.

"You asked for it, remember!"

I had to say, as much as I liked Trey the pussycat, there was something really enticing about Trey the tiger.

"So DO you think they know we just fucked?" Trey asked, nodding back to the old couple we'd just passed on the sidewalk.

"How do you know they haven't as well?"

Trey's face scrunched in disgust. "Ah! Old-people sex! Shit, man! Now I've got wrinkly dudes doing it in my head! Thanks for the image, Michael!"

We were heading for the Raven's Rest, although we were taking the scenic route. Trey needed to stop by the convenience store for cigarettes, and I needed a soda. After the séance, Mrs. Schultz had been afraid I'd just up and leave, especially after my statement that I was sleeping over at Trey's, but I'd assured her my absence would only be for the one night. She promised to have Lonnie fix the room back up before my return, although the only real damage had been to the blinds. The scratch on the table was there for good, much too deep to be repaired. Something told me that when, in a few days' time, I finally checked out of the Raven's Rest, the next guest would find a new table in place.

We were about to enter Casey's Convenience Store when someone emerged and Trey and I had to step back to allow them room.

It took me a moment to realize I'd seen the man before. He'd been the guy at McDonald's who had looked at me with shock on his face. And now that I thought about it, he'd asked if my last name was Finn.

As in Bryan Finn, Coleman Hollis's lover.

And again, the man's eyes grew wide as he saw me and Trey. "Excuse me," he muttered, and he barreled between us, making his way to an old pickup in the parking lot.

Trey just shook his head, excusing the man's rudeness, but I stood and watched as the man climbed into his vehicle. "Who is that guy? I've seen him before."

"Don't you know? That's Darryl Hollis. He used to own the property that's now the Raven's Rest. He was Coleman's father. I wonder how he'd feel if we told him we saw the ghost of his son last night."

"You're kidding! That's Coleman's...." I took a deep breath and let it out. "No wonder he asked if my last name was Finn. He knew Bryan, years ago. Seeing me must have dredged up some old memories."

Darryl Hollis was backing up, but we could see that his gaze hardly strayed from us as he maneuvered the truck. He didn't look happy.

"He always said that Coleman ran off, left town," Trey said. "We know he didn't."

"No. He died."

Hollis pulled out of the lot and gunned his engine as if he couldn't get away from us fast enough.

"I just got shivers up and down my spine," Trey said.

"Do you think he...?" I didn't need to finish the question.

Trey shrugged. "I wouldn't want to take any bets on it. I never did like that dude. Grouchy old bastard. Even Mom doesn't like him, and she likes everybody."

We bought Trey's cigarettes, and we both got Cokes. Back outside, we sipped as we resumed our walk. Trey lit up, his eyelids fluttering as he took his first drag.

"God, that's nearly as good as sex with you," he said.

"Thanks, I think."

"So what do you have on the agenda this afternoon?"

I swallowed some more Coke. "Well, I'd better find a furniture store and do some shopping. They've accepted my application, so if I'm moving into an apartment next week, I'll need some things. Like a bed. And somewhere to sit." The enormity of starting a life from scratch started to overwhelm me. "Shit! And a television! And what about cable? And I bet I have to get the electric bill switched to my name. And how am I going to pay for all this? My savings is—"

Trey laughed easily. "Don't worry, Michael! It'll all work out. Mom will pay you tomorrow, and—"

"That'll help, but it's going to cost—"

He punched me on the arm. "Relax! You know, you don't even have to go through with getting that apartment. Save up, if you need to."

"I can hardly afford to keep staying at the Raven's Rest."

Trey waggled his eyebrows. "You could always stay with me."

"Yeah, I'm sure your mom and your family would be thrilled with that."

"They'd love it! My mom loves you! Actually, much more than me." Trey frowned. "A lot more, now that I think about it. Hell, she might take you in and kick me out."

"I'm a little old to be moving into my boyfriend's family home," I said. "That's sort of... I don't know... high school, in a way."

Trey got a few paces in front of me and turned, strutting backward so he could taunt me.

"Oh, yeah, that's right! You're, like, a year and two months older than me! Quite the octogenarian!"

"Shut up or I'll throw your cigarette down and stomp on it."

"Got nineteen more, dude." He took a puff and blew it in my face, just to be an asshole. I still couldn't dislike him, even a little.

"Jerk," I said. "I don't suppose you'd like to go shopping with me?"

"Love to," he said, turning to face the right direction. "But I'm picking up a shift at the cafe. Won't be off until around eight." He kicked a pebble and watched it skip. "Sure you don't want to shack up together?"

"Not just yet. It's a little early. We just bumped uglies for the first time last night."

"Yours may be ugly. Mine's fucking gorgeous."

I chuckled. "It is, at that."

We were now within view of the Raven's Rest, and I could see a man walking up the porch steps. He was moving quickly and was inside the inn before I could get a really good gander at him, but something about the way he moved disturbed me, like I knew him. I didn't see the face, but his gait looked familiar. Tall, and with an athletic grace. I stopped, and Trey gave me a worried look.

"What's wrong?"

"Nothing." I shook my head. "Just… nothing. That guy seemed familiar."

"The guy who just went in? He's probably staying there. You've probably bumped into him in the hallway or something."

"Maybe," I said. I wasn't convinced. I shrugged off the sensation the guy had caused. "Hey, I'll swing by the cafe around eight if you like, and we can do something."

"Like?"

I grinned. "Let's go dancing. Is there a dance club in town?"

"Are you joking? In Banning? We could head up to Rockford—"

I stopped him there. "I'd rather not. Isn't there someplace that has a dance floor around here? Some bar with a juke box that doesn't have all country tunes?"

"There's Shooters, but…."

"What?"

"It's kind of a dive. Plus, a lot of good old boys hang out there. Two guys dancing? If we don't get doused by a dozen or so beers, we're sure to get the shit kicked out of us in the parking lot."

"Good point. We can go for a drink, though. Play it by ear."

"We could do that. Mind you, I don't mind getting in a fight. I'm just looking out for you."

"Of course you are."

Trey left me at the door, saying he wanted to get a shower before starting work. I wondered, however, if part of him was reticent to step foot back into the Raven's Rest so soon.

Lonnie was working the desk, and he grinned as he spotted me. "Mr. C! Hey, how's it going?"

"Going good, Lonnie."

"Ma told me about last night. I fixed your blinds. Damn, I wish I'd have been there. That's some funky shit."

"'Funky shit' isn't exactly how I'd put it."

I went upstairs to my room feeling pretty good, despite my money worries. Trey's mother wasn't paying me a fortune, but it would help. And really, all I needed to make my apartment livable was a bed and a chair and a television. Everything else could come piecemeal. I was eating most of my meals either at the cafe or in the Raven's Rest dining room, and anyway I'd never cooked much. The kitchen could wait. The main requirement was a bed big enough for me. And Trey, who I hoped would be spending lots of nights with me.

In the Ulalume Suite, things felt... odd. On the surface, everything was back to normal, except for the gouge in the table. The gas fire was off, the blinds were back in place, the books were neatly on the shelf, and the room had been vacuumed and the bed made. There were no cold spots, no dark shadows, and most importantly, no ghostly figures to be seen. There was something in the air, though, that I couldn't put my finger on. It was almost as if I could sense unseen forces gathering energy for something big, something huge.

I took a hot shower, more to relax than to cleanse myself. (Trey and I had shared a shower—and more—once we'd finally crawled out of bed.) Toweling myself off, I glanced at the mist-covered mirror, half expecting some word to be written there, like *Bryan* or *Coleman* or even REDRUM, like in the Stephen King story. There was nothing. I got dressed and read a chapter or two until I got drowsy. A nap seemed in order, so I lay down and, thankfully, got some uninterrupted and dream-free rest.

Later, I went to a furniture store in Sterling and picked out a bed and a nice little armchair and a couch. My checkbook balance at the end of this spree made me want to cry, but at the same time I felt liberated. By making purchases for my new place, I was proving to myself that I wasn't going to be running back to Kevin, begging forgiveness. I was really doing it. I was leaving him. And I was happy, mainly because each purchase made me envision Trey. Trey and me in the new bed. Trey and me snuggling on the couch, watching TV… once I bought one. Maybe I could find a used one cheap somewhere.

It was seven o'clock when I showed up at the Coffee Cafe. I knew Trey would still be working, but I wanted to take advantage of a free meal. My second day there, Trey's mother had said to me, "I can't pay you a fortune, but I can give you all the free food you want. Take advantage of it. God knows Trey does." And I'd accepted her hospitality almost every evening since, basically living off soup and sandwiches.

Of course, Trey waited on me, and he acted like I was a complete stranger, hardly looking at me as he asked for my order. "What would you like, sir?"

"How about the waiter?"

He swiveled his hips and slapped his thigh. "These goods don't come cheap, sir."

"That's not what I heard."

"Bitch."

"Slut. I'll have a ham sandwich and some chips." The menu wasn't extensive, as the place was mainly a coffeehouse, but the food wasn't really that bad. Trey snapped the menu out of my hands (I hadn't needed it anyway) and went off. Moments later, Gloria Ramsey came out from behind the counter and approached my little table by the window.

"Can I have a word?" she asked.

"Anytime."

She sat down and rested her chin on her fists. "So how did the shopping go?"

"How did you—"

Her smile was so similar to Trey's. "He talks about you. A lot." She sat back, reached into the pocket of her smock, and brought out an envelope. She slid it across the table toward me. "This is for you."

Frowning, I looked inside. There was money inside, at least ten bills. I didn't check, but a couple of them were fifties and at least one was a hundred. "What's this?"

"A bonus. Now, don't look like that. You deserve a bonus."

"Mrs. Ramsey—"

"Gloria."

"Gloria, then. No one gets a bonus in their first week of working somewhere. I can't accept this."

She sighed. "Trey's told me a little about your situation. I haven't been in exactly the same situation, but I know how hard it can be to start over. Take the money, kid. View it as a loan if you want. A loan that you can take years to repay, if ever. But take the goddamn money."

"I…." I almost returned the envelope to her, but I knew she'd insist I take it and that, in the end, she'd win. So I pocketed the cash without actually counting it. I'd do that later, and make sure every penny got back to her. "Thank you."

Gloria reached out and actually pinched my cheek. "You're part of the family now. Do you know Trey actually showed up on time today? And his clothes were clean? And his hair washed? Of course, he also had a Mona Lisa smile on his face, like a cat that finally snagged the canary. Not that I'm calling you a canary…."

I blushed. "I like Trey a lot. It's great that you're so supportive of him."

"What are you talking about? Of course I am. He's my son."

I thought of Darryl Hollis. "Not everyone is that accepting of their offspring's choices."

She looked like I was speaking nonsense. "How could anyone object to their kid dating you? Or not like a kid like Trey? Oh sure, he's a wastrel, and he likes to put on his surly tough-guy act, and he thinks he shocks people, but everyone sees through him. We just don't let him know that we all know he's a sweetheart." Gloria pursed her lips. "Did that sentence make sense?"

"Perfectly."

"Now, I'd best be getting back to work." She patted my hand. "You take care of yourself, honey. And don't forget, you've got an early shift tomorrow."

"Five in the morning. How could I forget?"

"So don't you and Trey stay up all night. Chatting, I mean." She flashed me a knowing look. There were two people waiting at the counter to pay their bill, so she rose from her chair. "I'm coming! I'm coming!" she exclaimed as she bustled across the dining room to take care of them.

Things were certainly different in a small town.

WE HAD the house to ourselves, as Trey's aunts and cousins were all out, and his mother was still at the cafe. So we took advantage of the situation.

Trey's room was a converted attic room and a little chilly, so after we made love we huddled under the covers, enjoying our shared body heat. And kissing. A hell of a lot of kissing.

"Okay," he said at one point, gazing into my eyes, "I'm thinking we're doing pretty good, right?"

"I'd say so. Good so far." Great, fantastic, superb. But I didn't want him to get a big head.

"So we should tell each other the worst things about ourselves. You know, the thing that sometimes puts people off. The deal breaker. If mine doesn't bother you and yours doesn't bother me, then we know we're made for each other."

"Okay." I grinned. "You go first."

"Why me?"

"You brought it up."

He conceded the point. "Right. But you can't laugh. And try not to go 'ewww.'"

"I'll try."

Trey sighed. "I've got a bit of an armpit fetish. Just a little one. And fuck, you've got bushy ones. And sometimes—you're laughing!—I just want to stick my face in them and... inhale. I know. Fuck, it's sick. I shouldn't have told you."

"No, it's good. And I wasn't laughing at you. Just... it's so you. I mean, it's pretty tame in the scheme of things. You're not into fisting or—"

"Fuck no!"

"Water sports or—"

"Ewww. Please tell me that's not yours. You wanna pee on me, I'm going to have to draw a line there. Now, what's yours?"

I thought a moment, leaning back into my pillow. "I think mine is that I lose myself in the other person. I cease to exist on my own. I become what the other person wants me to be, what he sees in me. I lose myself in their perceived perception of me. I think that's why I stayed with Kevin so long. I couldn't find myself. I was who he said I was, and without him I was afraid I wouldn't exist."

"Fuck," Trey said. "That's... fuck. That's... I almost wish it was water sports now. That I could deal with. Wait, don't look like that. I can deal with it, but you have to know that I'd never let you do that to yourself. I like you for you. Be you. You are a pretty good guy. Just believe in yourself."

"I know. Or I'm starting to. I just thought you ought to know." I looked at the clock on his bedside table and groaned. "Your family will be getting home soon. I'd better get dressed and get to the inn. I have to work early."

Trey held me tight, not letting me move. "Stay here tonight."

"I can't. You know I wouldn't get any sleep."

"Oh, yeah. Like you're going to get any sleep at Ghost Central."

I kissed him long and hard, then put a hand on his chest and pushed him gently away. "I've got to go," I said.

He pulled at my arm. "No! Stay!"

Laughing, I allowed him to yank me back into his arms. We wrestled around a little until he was on top of me. The covers were all tangled now, and we both were slightly aroused by the naked tussle. "A few more minutes," I said.

"Fuck that. An hour at least. Oh, don't think you're getting away. I'm smaller than you are, but stronger."

"Oh, you think so?"

More wrestling ensued, and he proved his point. Maybe he wasn't stronger, but he *was* more determined.

WE MET his mother on the stairs as Trey was showing me out. "I guess I don't have to ask what you boys have been up to," she said, her eyes twinkling.

"We were watching Netflix," Trey protested.

"Then why is your T-shirt on backward?" she asked.

He looked down and plucked at his shirt. "Oh. Shit."

Gloria playfully smacked his cheek. The unscratched one. "You'll always be my baby boy, even if you are a lazy asshole."

Trey smirked. "It's my thing."

We continued down the stairs, and Gloria yelled to me that she'd see me in the morning. I wondered if she ever got much sleep. She always seemed to be at the cafe.

The foyer was dark, but Trey didn't turn on any lights so that we could continue saying good-bye with a bit of privacy. When I finally realized we could stand there kissing until the end of time, I broke away and put my hand on the doorknob. "I'll see you tomorrow."

"You'd better. And no playing with the ghosts tonight. Get some sleep."

I put on my jacket and opened the door. One last kiss and I reluctantly turned away from Trey. As soon as I was outside, I missed him already. It was good to feel that way about a person again. I was grinning as I made my way down the steps.

I didn't even see the person standing on the sidewalk until I was only a few feet away from him. For one thing, he was standing in the shadows of the oak tree, out of the light from the streetlamp. But as I approached, he moved and spoke.

"So this is where you've been hiding yourself."

It was Kevin.

CHAPTER TWELVE

I FROZE, not believing my eyes.

"Kevin?"

"Come on. It's time to go home."

I couldn't seem to catch my breath. "What are you doing here?"

Kevin was wearing an old khaki jacket, torn jeans, and had a beanie clamped down over his short blond hair. He wasn't threatening me in any way, not physically, anyway. It was all in the attitude, in the way he carried himself and spoke. Kevin Anderson spoke, and Michael Cook obeyed. That was the way it always was. And dammit, part of me wanted to slip into that mode once again.

"I tracked you down," he said.

"How?"

He looked at me like I was stupid. I was used to that look. "Your cell phone. You can track someone by the GPS on their phone. It's really not even hard to do. Now come on. We're going to the Raven's Rest to collect your stuff."

I almost moved. Almost. I sucked in air instead and squared my shoulders. "How did you know I was staying at the Raven's Rest? How long have you been—" Realization dawned. "It was you following me the other night."

He nodded.

"My God," I muttered, anger rising within me. "How long have you been in Banning?"

"Just two days."

"And you've been stalking me."

A sneer found its way onto his lips, making his handsome face ugly. "I wanted to know just what you were up to. But now you've had your little fling. It's over. Time to come home."

"I don't think so," I said.

Kevin snorted. "Excuse me?"

"I can't go home. I'm already there. Banning is my home now."

Kevin grabbed me roughly by the arm. He wasn't big, but he was athletic. I tried to pull away, but he held me tight. "I've seen you," he said, "with that little scruffy guy. The long-haired fuckup from the cafe. Tell me, has he fucked you yet?"

"Leave Trey out of this," I said through gritted teeth as I attempted to break free of him. Kevin yanked at my arm, nearly throwing me off balance.

And then he hit me.

I didn't even see the punch coming. I wasn't expecting it, as he'd never done anything like that before. But my head flew back as his fist made contact with my chin and the pain jolted through me. I somehow managed to stay on my feet, and I quickly brought my hand up to my mouth to examine the damage. My fingers were smeared with red. He'd split my lip.

For just a second there was a look of fear in Kevin's eyes as he realized what he'd done. Then the steel returned. "You deserved that, you fucker. Now, unless you want me to beat the shit out of you, you'll get your ass in gear and collect your stuff from the inn. We're going home."

"What the hell is going on?" Trey's voice came from behind me. Apparently he'd looked out his window and seen an altercation was taking place. I turned to see him rushing down the steps, worry written on his face.

Kevin tried to grab hold of me again, but I jerked my arm out of his reach. To Trey he growled, "You keep out of this, you fucking hippie. This is between me and Michael."

Trey was at my side. He took one look at my bleeding face and then glared at Kevin. "You got a problem with Michael, you got a problem with me, asshole."

Shaking his head in mock wonder, Kevin said with a chuckle, "And that's supposed to scare me?"

"Just leave," Trey said. "We don't want any trouble."

He put his arm around me protectively. I'd have been proud of him if I wasn't so damned scared. I touched my bleeding lip and knew it was swelling. I stared at the back of my hand, now smeared with blood. In the feeble light it looked black, unreal. I had that coppery taste in my mouth and swallowed. That didn't help.

Kevin took a step toward Trey. "Out of the way, hippie." To me, he jerked his thumb vaguely in the direction of the Raven's Rest. "Come on. This is over. Get your ass back home."

"No," I said, surprising myself. Trey held me tighter, which gave me even more strength. "I'm through with you, Kevin. I'm sorry, but we just aren't a good fit. I'm staying here."

"You don't know what you're saying." It was typical Kevin logic. I was stupid; therefore, only he could know what was best for me. "You're letting this pretty little jerk turn your head, but what you're really doing is trying to punish me for some reason. Come back home. We'll discuss it."

"Good God, you don't listen, do you?" Trey exclaimed.

"Fuck off, you little bitch," Kevin said as he tried to push Trey aside so he could grab me.

Things moved rapidly after that, but to me it was as if they happened in slow motion. Trey rebounded from the shove and lurched forward to block Kevin from getting to me. Kevin's fist came up and slammed into Trey's nose. I screeched out Trey's name as he fell back. Kevin kept swinging, even as Trey tumbled to the ground. He crouched over Trey, pummeling him with lefts and rights. I tried to pin Kevin's arms to his sides, but he was too strong and too incensed. So I jumped up onto Kevin's back, which threw him off balance. He stumbled, and we went over.

And then I heard the whoop of a siren and saw the flashing blue lights of a squad car.

The cavalry had arrived.

WE WERE up in Trey's room. He was in his bed, looking miserable. We'd spent the last few hours at the hospital in Dixon as they saw to his nose, which the doctor informed us didn't need to be reset and would heal in time. Trey now had, however, a swollen nose, a cut on his chin, and two black eyes to accompany the scratches on his face.

They'd given him some pills for the pain, and he looked like he was barely awake as he forced a smile my way. "I almost had him, you know. Another couple of seconds, and he'd have been toast."

"Yeah," I said, grinning. "You're my knight in bruised and bleeding armor."

"What did Erin say? I missed all the fun of her hauling your jerk of an ex away, you know, with me lying there bleeding and everything."

"Deputy Hughes said he'll spend the night in jail at least. They're charging him with aggravated assault and several other things, I think even resisting arrest. She told me to get a restraining order as soon as possible."

"Can't they just shoot him and be done with it?"

"She thought that might be going too far." I was sitting on the edge of his bed, watching as his eyelids struggled to stay open. Even with bandages all over his face, I thought he was gorgeous. I stroked his forehead, as that was about the only unscathed spot. "You poor thing."

"Hey," he said groggily, "I'm a badass. Badasses don't require sympathy. We revel in our badassery."

"Well, now you've met Kevin."

"Yeah. And why were you with him for so long? Explain that to me. Because from where I'm sitting, he's not worth spitting at." Trey frowned. "Maybe that's what I should have done. Spit on him. Much better than fisticuffs."

"I wish I knew," I said, and then I kissed Trey's forehead. "I'd better go. You need to sleep."

"No, I'm good," he said, the words barely audible. "I...."

"You're almost asleep already."

"Yeah, you're right. Call me when you get up, okay?"

"You bet." I kissed him on the lips this time, although gently due to my own damaged face. I felt a little guilty. I came away with a cut lip, while Trey—basically an innocent bystander—had the crap beat out of him.

I crept downstairs to find several people in the foyer. Aunt Janet and Gloria Ramsey were there, with worried looks on their faces, listening to Deputy Erin Hughes, who was filling them in on the details. They all turned to me as I approached.

"How is he?" Gloria asked, a hand on her heart.

"Sleeping," I replied. "He insists he was just about to open up a can of whoop-ass on Kevin, and that if Deputy Hughes hadn't arrived when she did, Kevin would be in pieces by now."

"That's my son, the little asshole." She shook her head angrily. "If I get my hands on that guy, he'll wish he'd never stepped foot in this town." Flashing a guilty look at Erin Hughes, she added, "I'm just venting. Don't mind me."

The deputy nodded. "I understand. I'd feel the same way. Well, I'd best be going. Thanks for the coffee, Gloria. And you," she said, nodding at me, "get that restraining order. Tomorrow."

"I will." I took my jacket off the hook by the door, which elicited surprised looks from Janet and Gloria.

"You're staying here tonight, aren't you?" Janet asked.

"I'd like to, but I should sleep, which I won't do here. I've got to work—"

"Oh, honey." Gloria shook her head. "I'll get your shift covered. There's no way you're working in the morning. You go get a few hours of sleep and then come here and take care of Trey. Believe me, that'll be work enough."

I wasn't about to argue with her. The thought of getting up in a mere few hours and trying not to fall asleep while serving breakfast and coffee was too much to contemplate. "Thanks," I said.

"You need a ride?" Deputy Hughes asked.

"No, thanks. I'm good." And I was. My car was parked out on the street.

It took several more minutes before I could extricate myself from the Ramsey household, as both Gloria and Janet thought it was madness that I wished to spend the rest of the night—what little there was—in "that haunted house."

And, truth be told, I couldn't explain to them exactly why I felt the need to return to the Ulalume Suite, other than something inside my head was telling me I must. I wanted desperately to stay with Trey and to be there when he woke up in the morning, but something compelled me to return to the Raven's Rest.

It was nearly three in the morning when I used my key card to open the door of my room, and stepped inside. All was quiet. I arched an eyebrow and spoke to the empty room. "Coleman, are you here?" Feeling slightly silly, I tossed my keys onto the entertainment center and my jacket onto the back of a chair. Sitting down at the bottom of the bed, I took off my shoes and massaged my feet.

I hadn't really thought I'd get any sleep, but I found myself getting drowsy, so I went into the bathroom and switched on the light, intending to brush my teeth. First I examined my lip in the mirror. It was swollen and scabbing up, but it wasn't too bad. Certainly nothing compared to Trey's injuries. I smiled and said to my reflection, "You've got to stay with him now. He's been battered trying to defend you."

Guilt hit me. I should be at his side. Why had I come back here? What did I hope to accomplish? What did Coleman want me to know? That he and Bryan were dead? We knew that! How they died? Where they were buried? That made sense, but how could I find out if Coleman wouldn't tell me?

I prepared for bed and got under the covers, leaving just the light on the nightstand glowing. "Coleman," I said aloud, "I can only stay here two more days. After that, I'll be in my new apartment. So if you've got something to tell me, make it quick."

I didn't expect an answer, there not being the feeling that there was any supernatural presence in the room, and I didn't get one. I switched off the light and was asleep within minutes.

I DREAMED. I dreamed I was in my bed at the Raven's Rest, sleeping but not sleeping. Groggily, I sat up, suddenly fully awake. The room was darkened, but I could see a blue-tinted figure standing at the foot of the bed. Coleman Hollis. He was dressed in jeans and a T-shirt. There was the name of a rock band and their logo on the shirt, but it wasn't clear enough to make out. Rush? Led Zep? It didn't matter. The look on his face was wistful, slightly sad but yet not unhappy. His blond hair appeared white in the milky glow surrounding him.

I sat up. "Coleman?"

Yes. His lips didn't move, but I heard him nonetheless, as if the words were carried on a nonexistent breeze. His crooked smile grew. *You're not Bryan.*

"No," I answered, "but I'd like to help you find him."

The figure nodded. *So lonely.*

"Tell me what to do."

The blue-hued spirit seemed to frown. *So difficult. But I can show you.*

"I don't understand. What's difficult?"

Trying to tell people like this. Takes so much energy. Makes me weak. But I can show you, if you let me in.

"In? What do you mean?"

The figure moved, coming closer. Although *floated* would be a better description. The spirit approached me, his legs not moving at all, coming *through* the bed. The top of his legs just seemed to melt right into the mattress as he neared me. My left leg chilled as the ghost went through it. I hissed, feeling Coleman go right through first my foot and then my calf. He stopped, and I shifted so that no part of me was making actual contact with the spirit, who seemed oblivious to the reaction his touch produced.

He leaned over me. *I need to be with you. Inside your head. Then I can show you.*

I didn't like the sound of that. "You mean possess me?"

The spirit's sad eyes bore into me. *It's the best way. Then I can show you.*

"I want to help, but that's asking too—"

It will only be temporary. Just to show you. Please. I won't hurt you. You're a friend. I can tell that.

"I don't know."

Please. It's the only way.

I tried to reason it out. In a strange way, I knew I was dreaming, so did it matter if I agreed? Or was Coleman actually visiting me in my dream? If I let him possess me, would I awake as myself or Coleman or a combination of the two of us?

My mind was screaming at me to say no, that this was too risky. My heart, however, was telling me that I needed to help this young man, even if he was long dead. I'd said I would. And if this was the only way to find out why he was haunting the Raven's Rest, shouldn't I give it a try? As long as it was only temporary? I thought of Trey, who'd gone through so much for me. Getting scratched, getting beaten. He was ready to protect me, to do whatever it took to keep me safe. Maybe Coleman needed someone to take a risk for him.

"Okay," I whispered.

The spirit nodded and then floated closer. Suddenly he was on top of me, although there was no weight, just a massive chill that made me shudder. For a brief moment I could see his face close to mine, mere inches away. Now I could see the green of his eyes, and his long blond hair fell forward, touching my cheek like dry icicles. It almost seemed like he was about to kiss me, but then my body convulsed and I gasped as he melted into me.

At first I couldn't even breathe. It felt like I'd jumped off the deck of the *Titanic* into the icy water, and the shock was intense. Slowly, warmth crept back into my bones, and I sucked in a grateful lungful of air.

My mind raced, and I saw visions. Playing superheroes with my friends as a child, a red blanket pinned onto my back as I soared across the front lawn, making *whooshing* noises to indicate flying. Watching cartoons in the living room in my pj's while scooping in mouthfuls of cereal. Older, riding my bicycle through town, my buddy Scott pedaling beside me. I wondered how he would feel if I told him I had a crush on him? Older still, mowing the lawn and hoping to catch sight of the new boy next door. His name was Bryan, and he was the handsomest boy I'd ever seen.

And later, becoming friends and then more with Bryan. Our first kiss, one night out by the gazebo, with snow falling and the air crisp and clean as his breath. There were Christmas lights on nearby, not only my house but our neighbors as well. Mr. Martin's house across the way was lit up like a beacon, and his roof was adorned with a plastic Santa on a sleigh being pulled by four plastic reindeer, which always bothered me. Didn't everyone know there had been eight reindeer, or nine if you counted Rudolph? But I couldn't care less about the disparity of reindeer as long as Bryan held me close, allowing me to explore his wonderful mouth with my tongue.

And later still, making love with Bryan one afternoon in my room. There was a smile on my face as I pistoned my hips into him, and he groaned with pleasure. "Oh God, I love you," he moaned as he shot his semen onto his belly. The mere sight of the ecstasy on his face made me come as well.

Another scene, a breakfast with my father. He had a cross look on his face, which wasn't unusual, and I knew he was hungover from the booze he drank the night before. "I don't like that Bryan kid," he said, not daring to look me in the eyes. "I don't think you should see him anymore. People say he's a fruit."

"Like a pear? Or a peach?" I retorted hotly, so mad my ears feel like they're on fire. "Maybe a plum?"

"Don't be facetious," he growled. "You know what I mean. If you hang around with his sort, people will start to talk. They'll start to wonder about you."

"I don't care if they do," I reply.

"Well, I do! No son of mine is going to be a faggot!"

More thoughts hit me. More feelings. A funeral. My mother's. Father was there, swaying as the minister said a few words at the grave site. Dad was drunk, not that that surprised me, or anyone else there for that matter. Ever since Mom had been diagnosed with lung cancer, the bar down the road had become his second home. Maybe his first.

And then the night he punched me because he'd seen Bryan and I kissing each other good night. We'd thought he was at the bar, but he had been sitting in the dark in the living room and had spotted us on the porch.

That was the night Bryan and I had plotted our escape.

I blinked as I sat up in bed. Visions, memories, but they weren't *my* memories. They were Coleman's. And I wasn't dreaming. I was wide awake. The sun was coming up, the light creeping in through the gaps in the blinds. I shook my head, and the kaleidoscope of daydreams ceased. Or at least they receded. Closing my eyes tight, I swore under my breath, wondering just what the hell I'd done, what I'd allowed to happen.

Because Coleman Hollis was there, somewhere. In my mind. I could feel him.

My stomach churned, and I rushed out of bed, hoping I could reach the toilet before I threw up. I fumbled for the light switch, retching. I knew I had only seconds, not enough time to hit the toilet bowl, so I bent over the sink and gagged. I was there for what seemed like ages, splattering the porcelain with my vomit, although it was probably only seconds. My skin felt cold and clammy, and beads of perspiration dripped off my forehead.

When nothing more would come up, I stayed bent over the counter, afraid my legs wouldn't hold me up on their own. Finally I had enough energy to turn on the taps to wash as much of my sick away as I could.

I looked up into the mirror, and for a moment it wasn't my face reflected there. It was Coleman Hollis's. I blinked, and the image became my own. But was there something of Coleman remaining? My own eyes were more of a hazel tint, but now they were definitely green. Just like Coleman's.

"My God, Michael," I asked myself, "what have you done?"

CHAPTER THIRTEEN

"WHY IS it that I'm the one that got the shit knocked out of me, but it's you who looks like hell?" Trey asked.

Truth be told, neither of us was at our best, but my casualties were limited to puffy, dark eyes from very little sleep (hopefully Trey hadn't noticed the different pigmentation) and a busted lip, while Trey had multiple cuts, plus two black eyes. I ignored his question and asked, "How are you feeling?"

He was in his bed and sat up slowly, pondering. "It's odd," he said at last. "I hurt in places that asshole didn't even hit me. Like my back. It hurts like a motherfucker. And my neck. The spots that he actually hit? They're all kind of numb still. Just dull aches."

"Here. Lean forward." He did so, and I sat beside him and began to massage his neck and shoulders. "Better?"

He grunted.

"Too hard?" I asked.

"No, it's heaven. Don't stop."

I moved his long hair to one shoulder so I could get at his neck better. He hung his head low to stretch out the muscles. I kissed his shoulder and then continued to dig my fingers into his skin. "Let me know if I hit a sore spot."

"They're all sore. That bastard's just lucky he caught me off guard."

I smiled, thankful Trey couldn't see me and think I was grinning at his expense. Under any circumstances, Trey wouldn't have fared well against Kevin, but I wasn't about to point this out. Trey was my protector and hero, no matter how ineffectual that was in practice. It still made me love him just a little bit more.

"Trey?"

"Yeah?"

Tell him. Tell him what you did. Let him know. But the words wouldn't come out. At the moment, my mind was totally my own. There were no stray feelings or memories from Coleman in my head, but I had no idea whether they'd remain at bay. And Coleman was in there, somewhere, resting up to reveal more to me. I knew that. It felt like he was close by, like a person sitting next to you at a crowded movie theater. You knew they were there, even if they weren't actually making contact with you. But then they shifted, and their elbow hits yours, or you knocked your hand against their sleeve.

What I did say seemed to just burst out, without much thought on my part. "I think I'm falling in love with you."

I couldn't see his mouth, but I sensed his grin. "Good thing," he joked, "'cause with my face all battered, no one else is gonna want me." He paused and then said, in a serious tone (the most serious I'd heard him use), "I'm falling for you too. Actually, fallen. But I've always been impulsive. Hand me my ciggies, would you?"

I grabbed the pack off his nightstand. "I thought your mom didn't like you smoking in the house."

"That was before I went a round with Rocky Balboa. I ain't going outside looking like this."

I stopped rubbing his back and put my head on his shoulder. "I'm so sorry," I said.

"Why? You didn't punch me."

"You know what I mean."

My hand was on his other shoulder, and he reached up and patted it. Sighing, he said, "I have to admit, I'm a little scared."

"You don't have to be. Kevin will never touch you again. I'll make sure of it."

Trey snorted. "Not him! I'm not scared of that dipshit! No, I meant the other shit that's going on. The ghosts."

"What about them?" I asked, guilt welling inside me.

"I'm worried about you. You're out of there on Monday, right?"

"Thereabouts. Depends on how fast I can get the furniture delivered. The lease is all signed, though."

"The sooner the better," Trey said. "Something tells me that you're in danger. I don't know exactly how, but I think you'll be safer living somewhere other than the Raven's Rest."

"Funny. Jesenia Maupin said pretty much the same thing. That I was in danger there."

Trey shrugged. "Maybe she's not as crazy as I thought she was." He threw back the covers and made motions as if he was getting up.

"What are you doing?" I asked.

He gave me a you're-an-idiot look. "It appears that I'm getting out of bed. My morning wood has gone down a bit, but feel free to reignite its passions if you wish. But then I'm going to take a shower, and we're going out for breakfast."

"It's nearly eleven, and shouldn't you stay in bed today and rest?"

Trey frowned. "I got punched a few times. I'm not broken. Other than a slight headache, I'm fine." He was wearing nothing but his underwear. Black, of course. And despite his statement, the material wasn't tented in the slightest. Not yet, anyway.

I put a restraining hand on his thigh. "Stay where you are, Trey."

"I'm fine. Really."

"I didn't mean that," I said as I gently pushed him back against his pillow while my other hand fumbled with the waistband of his boxers.

"Oh," he replied with a smile.

"Yeah, oh."

My mouth was full after that, so I didn't talk much for the next few minutes.

TREY, DRESSED in his usual black T-shirt and jeans and a black leather jacket, lit up a cigarette as we approached McDonald's, automatically slowing his pace so he could enjoy a sufficient amount of nicotine before we reached the entrance. In the bright light of day, his injuries didn't look quite as bad. My own lip was still puffy but starting to heal nicely.

My other affliction, that of having a spirit inside me, was another matter. I could still feel Coleman's presence there in my brain, resting up. It was an odd sensation, having another consciousness inside my head. I knew I should tell Trey, but to be honest, I was afraid of his reaction. When I imagined telling him, he would listen quietly and then tell me how stupid I'd been. And while I couldn't argue with that assessment, it hit too close to home. In my scenario, Trey's voice morphed with Kevin's as he said, "God, Michael, I can't believe how idiotic you can be sometimes." I couldn't take that.

So I kept mum.

"Good cigarette?" I asked instead.

Trey smiled as he exhaled smoke. "You don't like me smoking, do you?"

"Of course not. It's a nasty habit."

He shrugged. "Maybe I can give it up sometime. Maybe."

"I'll wait with bated breath," I replied with a chuckle.

He tossed the cigarette butt to the pavement and stomped on it with his boot. We went inside, and I glanced around at the patrons, half hoping that Jesenia Maupin would be among them. She wasn't, but I knew that sooner or later I'd be seeking her out for advice.

The girl at the counter who took our order knew Trey and, concerned, asked what happened to his face. I could tell the words just came out and she was unaware how tactless her question might have been.

"Got into a fight with his ex," Trey explained, nodding toward me. "You should see him."

As we carried our trays to a table, I asked Trey about his last statement.

"I just said she should see him," he said with his Mona Lisa grin. "I didn't say he looked worse than me. Although I'm way hotter than he is. Even with the cuts and bruises."

"You are," I agreed. There had been a time, I knew, when I'd thought Kevin was the handsomest man on the face of the planet. Unfortunately, the man's personality seeped into my perception of his looks after a while, and now I always pictured Kevin with a nasty sneer on his lips and anger in his eyes. Trey, however, was beautiful even with his injuries. I fought the urge to cover his face with kisses as we sat down.

I froze with my butt just inches away from settling onto the chair. At a nearby table was Darryl Hollis, sitting with another man. They were deep in conversation and hadn't noticed us.

Alarm bells went off in my skull, and I was filled with a seething anger at the mere sight of the man. I knew these were the feelings of Coleman Hollis, but at the moment they were indistinguishable from my own.

"What?" Trey asked, noticing my imitation of a statue. He followed my gaze. "Oh, him. Take no notice." When I still didn't move, he added, "Eat a french fry or something. You're scaring me."

That broke the spell. I shook my head, back to my old self, although my neck seemed stiff and sore, and there was a low throbbing in my temples. Ah, the things they don't tell you about possession! I wished I could share my thoughts with Trey. I yearned to. Instead I rubbed the back of my head, massaging the tense muscles. "I'm okay," I said.

"Really? Because you're acting like... I don't know what you're acting like. Weird. Did you get any sleep?"

"Not much. You?"

"I was on pain pills. Slept like a log."

"How's your nose?"

Trey touched it lightly. "Tender. I can breathe through it, though. That's the important thing. Your ex is an asshole."

"You're not telling me anything I hadn't already figured out myself." I began to eat, but every now and then I found myself looking over at Darryl Hollis, and I felt a little shiver run down my spine every time. "Who's that with him?"

Trey half turned. "With Hollis? That's Gary Thornton. Used to be sheriff here, years ago."

"Was he sheriff at the time Coleman supposedly disappeared?"

"Maybe. I guess so. Before my time, that's all I know. Nowadays, like old Darryl, he sits at the Roadhouse Tavern and drinks himself into oblivion most nights."

"I wonder what they're trying to forget."

"Maybe they just like alcohol. Or," Trey said, narrowing his eyes, "they both were involved in killing Coleman and Bryan." When my eyes widened in surprise, Trey continued, a bit loudly, "What? We're both thinking it!"

"Shh!"

Hollis and Thornton had both turned their heads our way.

In low tones, Trey said, "You can't be a ghost without being dead. And if Bryan and Coleman disappeared at the same time, that indicates foul play. And that rumor about Coleman meeting some gal and getting married is pure bullshit. No, Coleman and Bryan were most likely murdered. Even if Thornton wasn't directly involved, I bet he helped Darryl cover up the crime. At the very least, he hushed the whole thing up and told people that the two simply left town, when he knew damn well that they were dead."

"And they're, like, four feet away from us." My head was buzzing, though. Coleman was trying to tell me something, but all I was really getting from him was waves of hatred. I closed my eyes, feeling a little sick to my stomach.

"So? You want things stirred up, don't you? I'm sure Coleman would."

Darryl Hollis's head jerked up. I was sure he overheard Trey saying his son's name. The man turned his head slightly, eyeing us with a frown.

But Trey was right. Coleman was pleased with the reaction. I could tell.

THAT AFTERNOON a nap I was taking was interrupted by a call from Betty Schultz, telling me that Deputy Sheriff Hughes was downstairs and wanted to have a word with me. I thanked her and quickly made my way downstairs. Erin Hughes was standing by the front desk, wearing a heavy coat and a stern expression.

"Shall we sit in the solarium a moment?" she suggested. "I want to fill you in on what's happening."

I didn't feel like sitting, so I perched on the edge of a wicker chair and clasped my hands together tightly to keep them from shaking. Hughes tried a reassuring smile, but she gave up on it quickly.

"He's out, isn't he?" I said.

She nodded. "He's been instructed to come nowhere near you or Trey. He'd been checked in here at the Raven's Rest, but he's packed up and left now. Presumably he's gone back to Rockford. I want you to call me if you see him, or even if you hear from him. Phone calls, anything. Hell, if he leaves you a nasty message on Facebook, I want to hear about it."

So Kevin had been staying here at the inn. He must have been the guy in the Raven Suite. It chilled me to think he'd been just down the hall. I sighed deeply. "Thanks for telling me."

"How's Trey?" Hughes asked.

I managed a smile. "He's acting like he's invincible, of course. When people tell him he looks like he's been in a fight, he answers that they should see the other guy. So he's being Trey. All five foot seven of skinny badass toughness. Or at least that's what he'd like people to think."

"That sounds like Trey. And you?"

I exhaled slowly and sat back. "Oh," I said, "I can honestly say I've never felt quite like this."

I could tell Hughes didn't know what to make of this statement. I wasn't sure myself.

OVERALL, I felt okay. Weird but okay. Most of the time I could even forget that Coleman Hollis was somewhere in my brain, or wherever he was. I felt a little sluggish, drained, as if I'd just finished some strenuous exercise. My right eye felt funny, like that eyelid was heavier than the left one, and occasionally I found myself trying to use my left hand as the dominant one. Coleman must have been left-handed. And still, when I looked in a mirror, I first saw Coleman's reflection, which quickly morphed into my own.

I took a long hot bath late that afternoon and lazed in the water as I pondered my situation. I knew I had to tell Trey, or somebody. Yes, he'd tell me I'd been foolish, but I had been. Trey, however, wouldn't hold it against me like Kevin would. So I'd take my lumps and spill my guts.

After getting out of the tub and toweling off, I padded naked into the bedroom and called Trey to see if he'd like to get together.

"Let me check my busy social calendar," he answered. "Oh, look. I'm free. What a coincidence. Wrote a new song, by the way. You get to listen to it before we head out and find something to do. If it sucks, don't tell me."

"I'm sure it doesn't," I assured him before hanging up.

I hadn't shaved in the morning, not wanting to gaze into the mirror at the time, so I lathered up and scraped a razor across my cheeks. My lip was healing nicely but was still tender, so I took extra care shaving around my mouth. I'd done half my face before I realized I was using my left hand. I stared at it, gripping the disposable razor.

"Coleman, show me what you need to show me and get the hell out," I muttered. I braced myself and then peered into the mirror. My reflection. My right eye twitched, but that was my only sign from the spirit within me.

In movies, when someone gets possessed, they go around hacking people to death with an ax, or spewing pea soup and doing three-hundred-and-sixty-degree head turns. The original personality is completely dominated by the new entity. I wasn't finding that the case, thankfully. Not that I thought Coleman was a murderous type.

And what was he experiencing? When I looked in the mirror, what did Coleman's consciousness see? Did he see himself, foam all over his face, ready to be shaved? Did he see his eyes looking back at him? Or did he see the man who so resembled his old boyfriend, Bryan Finn?

And what had happened to Bryan Finn, anyway? Why couldn't his spirit be with Coleman?

Maybe Jesenia Maupin would know. I made a mental note to contact her first thing in the morning.

I finished shaving with my right hand and dressed. Jeans, a light blue shirt, and a brown pullover sweater. After donning a heavy jacket, I made my way downstairs, first pausing to listen at the door to the Raven Suite. No sounds came from within. Good.

Outside, Lonnie Schultz was taking down the Halloween decorations. He was trying to stuff a battery-operated witch into an already overstuffed box when he saw me emerging.

"Hey, Mr. C! How are things today?"

"Better than yesterday," I answered.

"Yeah, heard about that. Exes are a bitch, aren't they?"

"Truer words were never spoken, Lonnie." Something clicked in my mind. "That scrapbook you showed me. The one with the pictures of Coleman Hollis in it. Do you think I could see if again?"

He shrugged. "Sure. I don't think there are any other pictures of Coleman, though."

"But there are some of the house before it became the Raven's Rest?"

"Oh, sure. Loads."

"I'd like to see them, if I may."

"I can get it for you now, if you like." I thought any excuse to stop packing up decorations would have been welcome to Lonnie.

I shook my head. "I'm off to see Trey. Tomorrow morning will be fine."

Lonnie nodded as he picked up a foam tombstone. "I'll be sorry to see you go, Mr. C. I've enjoyed our chats."

"I'll still be in town, Lonnie. Just down the street, really. And I'll be working at the cafe. You can always drop in and see me there."

"Might just do that, Mr. C. You take care now."

I went down the porch steps slowly, as I was feeling a bit uneasy. I had nothing to base my fears on other than a niggling at the base of my spine. I'd never been prone to premonitions, but this one turned out to be accurate. When I got to my car in the parking lot, something immediately looked off-kilter, and it soon was obvious that my back left tire was flat. I squatted down and examined it, as if that would help. As if I could will air back into the stupid thing. I sighed and stood up, rubbing the back of my neck to ease the tension building there. The tire was fairly new, and I hadn't had any trouble with it previously. Had I run over a nail or something? Did that even deflate tires nowadays?

Lonnie must have seen me standing there looking like a damsel in distress because the next thing I knew his voice sounded behind me, startling me a little.

"Damn, man. That is one flat tire."

I smiled wryly and went to open the trunk. "Well, now we get to see if I can change a tire without killing myself." I blinked as I looked at the debris in front of me. I saw an empty box that had been there since Christmas, a John Grisham paperback, jumper cables that I'd never used, and some other junk. No tire. "Where is it?"

Chuckling, Lonnie moved me out of the way and shoved the jumper cables aside. "Under here, my man." He showed me there was a flat of carpeting covering the well where the spare was stored. A frown crossed his face. "Unfortunately, it's flat as well."

Now I recalled that the tire that was now flat had been replaced (by Kevin) sometime in the spring and at that time he'd warned me that my spare needed air. I groaned in disgust. "Is there anywhere in town that can fix this?" I asked as I kicked the offending tire.

"Sure, several places." Lonnie was trying his best to seem encouraging. "Roscoe's is the closest. I'd have him tow you in, and he can get you fixed up in a flash."

"Tonight?" I asked hopefully.

Lonnie sucked in air with a wet hiss and shook his head. "First thing in the morning, though. Want me to call him?"

"Please."

Lonnie spoke to Roscoe himself, but his prediction that I'd have to wait until morning held true. He ended the call and said, "If you need a ride…."

"I'm just going to Trey's. I can walk."

Lonnie, still holding a plastic skeleton, seemed dubious. "If you're sure."

I wasn't, to be honest. The flat tire worried me, as I wasn't altogether sure it was a mere flat tire. Had someone deliberately let the air out or slashed it? I could see no obvious slices in the rubber, but that didn't mean much. And with Kevin out of jail, anything was possible. It was just the sort of petty thing he'd do. Supposedly he'd left town, but what if he was waiting for me somewhere, such as down the street?

On the other hand, I was anxious to see Trey, and if I got a ride from Lonnie I'd first have to wait for him to go in and let his mother know and get his keys. By that time, I could be halfway to Trey's house.

"I'm good," I said, but it wasn't me who spoke.

My voice must have sounded odd to Lonnie, because he shot me a curious glance. "You got our number if you need anything, right?"

"Sure do." That was me. Everything was back to normal. But why had Coleman suddenly spoken up?

I began walking and pondered as I went. I tried to search my mind, to sense Coleman's presence there, but it had retreated just as suddenly as it had emerged. He had wanted me to go on foot, or so it seemed. Why?

Reaching the corner, I began to feel a little less worried. Night was falling and the skies were overcast, but there were lots of lights on in the houses along the way, and every now and then I could see people inside, going about their business. If Kevin was lying in wait, I had options. Just in case, I got my cell phone out of my pocket and kept it in my hand after punching in 911. A touch of the Send button would bring law enforcement officials in a matter of minutes.

I continued to walk, and once again tried to access the part of my brain where I felt Coleman was residing. *Why did you want me to walk instead of accepting a lift?* I asked silently.

There was no direct reply, but I did get a feeling like he was trying to tell me something. He just didn't have the energy, or maybe he was adjusting to the possession, same as I was.

And then I felt compelled to slow my pace. It was certainly an odd feeling, like my legs suddenly were leaden, and a sharp pain at the base of my neck made me cry out. Okay, Coleman was trying to tell me something, but what? I looked around. On my left, across the street, were modest little houses, most of them lit, as the families within were getting ready for dinner or to settle down to watch some television. On my right was a vacant lot, and slightly ahead of me was an old building that had once been a record store. Now it was derelict, with rotting timbers and broken windows.

No, it wasn't the building Coleman was trying to draw my attention to. The vacant lot?

It was like a buzzer went off in my brain. Bingo.

But what was there that Coleman wanted me to see? All I could make out was overgrown grass, what looked like a patch where some kids had attempted to make a baseball diamond and given up, and some discarded junk—a tire someone had left, lots of broken glass and bottles, and a rusted bicycle that looked like it had been lying untouched in the dirt for decades.

An image sprang to my mind, a memory. It just wasn't my memory.

Coleman and Bryan were walking out of Marty's Record Shop, only now it wasn't a deserted wreck. The building was painted a deep russet, and there was a lit sign hanging over the door with the shop's name, promising great deals on the latest releases. Bryan had a slim package in his hands, and the two young men were laughing and jostling each other as they walked. Bryan opened his paper package and pulled out a record album. I recognized the cover as Pink Floyd's *Dark Side of the Moon*. They were talking, but I couldn't hear what they were saying. Coleman pointed to something on the album and made a comment and Bryan laughed.

They were a cute couple, I thought to myself, and they were so obviously in love, but I was a little surprised they weren't toning down their affection while they were out in public. Surely they were a bit brazen for a small town in the 1980s. They had my admiration, but I couldn't help but feel a pang of worry for them.

And considering they both vanished without a trace, my concern wasn't misguided.

They approached the spot where I was standing, obviously not seeing me. It was a vision, after all. I wasn't really there. But as Bryan came closer, his image began to fade. When the couple was only a few feet away from me, the smiling Bryan—my twin from another era—was barely visible at all. They came abreast of me, and suddenly Coleman was walking alone. He glanced at me—no, at the vacant lot behind me—with a look of unbearable sorrow. And then he too disappeared from sight.

I blinked. The record shop was again abandoned and dark. No spirits roamed the streets, and a chill ran up and down my spine. Coleman's presence had retreated once again into the inner recesses of my mind.

I looked back at the field and shivered again, although I was not quite sure why.

Still pondering my vision, I started to cross the street. So engrossed was I in my thoughts that I didn't hear the roar of the engine until the car was nearly upon me.

I froze, practically in the middle of the street, as a dark vehicle, tires screaming, raced right toward me.

CHAPTER FOURTEEN

I DOVE, hitting the pavement hard. Rolling, I was aware of a flurry of motion at my side as the speeding car missed me by mere inches. There was a squeal of brakes, and I thought at first that the driver was stopping to see how I was. My eyes were closed from pain, however, and I barely heard the engine gunning again and the resulting protest from the tires. The driver sped away.

I gasped and cradled my right arm, which had taken the brunt of the fall. My jacket was scraped and torn, and my elbow felt like it was on fire. I shifted, just to make sure that I could still move, and a jolt of pain ran through me. My right leg hurt as well, as did my shoulder. There were tears in my eyes as I heard people approaching rapidly. People from one of the neighborhood houses had obviously witnessed the near hit and were coming to offer aid. Stupidly, however, my first thought—other than wishing the agonizing pain would go away—was the location of my cell phone. It had been in my hand and had gone flying.

My brain was muddled, and I know I cried out as I rolled over onto my back. Someone—a male voice—warned me not to move. I could see faces huddled over me. A young couple, a dark-haired guy with facial stubble and a very worried-looking woman with long blonde hair. Behind them was a kid, maybe six or seven years old. He seemed disappointed there was no visible blood.

I started to sit up, but the guy placed a hand on my shoulder. "Stay still," he said. "Let's make sure you're okay before you start moving around."

The woman had moved off a few paces, and at first I thought she was speaking into her hand. That's how befuddled I was. Finally it dawned on me that she was on her phone. "That's right," she said. "Whoever it was *tried* to run him over. The car's lights were off!"

She was right, although I hadn't realized it at first, being much too occupied with the horrifying thought that a car was speeding toward me. There had been no headlights, even though we were well into dusk.

"Kevin," I muttered.

The young man with the chin stubble frowned at me. "Is that your name?"

"No, it's my ex. That must have been who tried to run me over. Kevin Alexander."

He passed this information along to the woman, and she in turn told the police. Another jolt of pain shot through my arm, so I didn't pay much attention to what she was saying. The guy, though, was right in my face, so it was hard to ignore him.

"Does this hurt?" he said, touching my leg.

"No," I said. Mostly it was my hip. I shifted my leg to show the guy it wasn't broken. He allowed me to sit up. I winced, holding my arm tight against my chest. Everything was blurry. "My glasses."

"Here they are!" The kid held them up like a prize he'd found.

I put them on. They felt crooked on my face, but at least things were in focus now.

My jeans were torn at the knee, showing a big scrape and some blood. The arm of my jacket had remained intact, but it was streaked and dirty where it had come into contact with the asphalt. I felt woozy.

And odd. Somehow, I knew Coleman Hollis was no longer within me.

More realizations came to me. Just before the car had nearly plowed into me, I'd felt the spirit vacate my body, and forceful hands had pushed me out of the way.

Coleman Hollis had probably saved my life.

THE NEXT morning, Erin Hughes came to see me at the cafe. Despite my injuries (or, perhaps, because of them) I refused to call off work. Granted, I was stiff, I limped slightly, and I had to use my left hand more than usual, but under the circumstances I think I did okay. I have to admit, though, that I was more than happy to see Ms.

Hughes. Gloria allowed me to take a break and sit down with her for a few minutes.

"It wasn't your ex," she said as soon as she settled into her chair. "We checked. He was definitely in Rockford last night."

That didn't make sense. "It had to be him," I insisted. "Who else would want to try to kill me?"

The deputy shook her head. "I don't know, but Kevin Alexander was at work last night. His boss at the Cracker Barrel said he was on duty his whole shift, from three until ten thirty."

My brush with death had taken place around seven o'clock.

"I thought for sure it was him."

"You said you didn't recognize the car," she reminded me.

True, but I'd assumed he'd borrowed one. Any of Kevin's buddies would have swapped vehicles for the night. All he'd have to do was give them some lame excuse. But if Kevin hadn't tried to run me over, who did?

"Could he have hired someone to do it?" I asked.

"Possible, I suppose," Erin said. She didn't sound like she thought it likely. And to be fair, how would Kevin know how to find a hit man? It wasn't like he could locate a hired killer on Craigslist. "Are you sure there isn't anyone else that would want to harm you?"

"I can't imagine who," I replied.

"It may have just been someone who didn't know you at all."

"Some random crazy?" I asked.

She smiled gently. "It does happen. Even in little burgs like this one."

I arched an eyebrow. "Oh? And has anything similar happened in Banning before?"

Erin Hughes had to admit it hadn't. "We'll keep looking into it," she assured him. "And I haven't ruled anything out, even your ex." She shifted gears, going from cop doing her job to a friend. "How are you doing?"

"I was pretty lucky, really. Just some nasty scrapes and bruises. They checked me out at the hospital in Dixon, but nothing was broken except my cell phone. That didn't survive. They prescribed some lovely pills for the pain, though."

"You and Trey have been keeping me busy. Stop it, will you? I want you guys to stay in one piece."

I peered into the opening in the back wall into the kitchen, where Trey was making sandwiches for the lunch crowd. "We'll try."

"Do more than try." Good advice. I just wished it were that easy. "I understand you're moving out of the Raven's Rest tomorrow."

I nodded. "My furniture is supposed to be here in the morning. I called the store this morning and they confirmed delivery."

Erin smiled. "Well, I guess this means you're officially a resident of Banning now."

"I guess I am."

She leaned back, a look of concern on her face. "I'm serious, though, about you staying safe. You've pissed someone off, it seems. Enough that they tried to run you over."

"I have every intention of watching my back from now on."

I wondered what Erin Hughes would say if I told her that I was sure I'd escaped getting hit only due to the intervention of a ghost. Best, I thought, not to find out.

TREY WASN'T happy about my decision. "Someone tried to kill you last night, and you want to go somewhere by yourself?"

"It's broad daylight!" I protested. "And it's just to Jesenia Maupin's place."

"I still don't like it."

I wasn't entirely at ease myself, but I wanted to see Jesenia alone. If anyone had answers to my questions, it was her. And as I hadn't yet told Trey about my possession—if that was what it even had been—by Coleman, I didn't want him finding out through my conversation with Jesenia. "It's just a few blocks over—"

"Yeah, well, everything is just a few blocks over. It's a small town." Trey and I were in the kitchen, still leaning over the huge sink, having just finished loading the last of the dirty plates, mugs, and cutlery into the dishwasher. The water we'd used to hose off the knives and forks had been so hot that the basin was still sending up wafts of steam, even though the taps were now off.

"It'll be fine. And my car's fixed now. New tire and everything." Even though it was a Sunday, Roscoe's Garage had worked on my car and even delivered it to the parking lot of the cafe. I'd tried to tip the big, burly shop owner, but he'd refused to take any money. My first trip in the repaired vehicle had been to purchase a new cell phone.

"I don't care." Trey's arms were folded across his chest, and his face was set in stone. "In the last few days, we've both been beaten by your stupid ex-boyfriend. Before that, I was scratched by something that wasn't there! And last night, he tried to run you over—"

"Deputy Hughes says it couldn't have been—"

Trey snorted. "Yeah. I'll believe that when it's proved beyond a doubt, which will be never. Who else would it have been? You don't even know that many people in town. And while a customer may not tip you big if you don't remember to refresh his coffee every five minutes, rarely do they attempt to run you over. As far as I'm concerned, you're going nowhere without me."

In a way, I was pleased about his protectiveness. But only in a way. I turned to him, staring into his eyes to let him know how important my words were. I touched his cheek tenderly. "Trey, I know you mean well, but don't try to be too controlling. It kind of reminds me of Kevin, and—"

He gasped. "Oh no! I didn't mean to—"

"I know you didn't. And I know there's a difference. Kevin's demands were all about power over me. Yours were out of concern. But if we're going to be boyfriends, you're going to have to let me have some space. You're going to have to know I'm going to make mistakes. And you're going to have to accept that I'm going to be scared to tell you some things. I hid so much from Kevin, knowing how he'd react."

"But I'd never—"

I kissed him, cutting off his protests. My lip was still slightly swollen, but at least kissing caused no pain. Quite the opposite, in fact. "I know." I breathed in and let the air out slowly. "I have to see Jesenia alone. You see, I did something foolish, reckless. It turned out okay, and it's over now, but I can't tell you about it yet. I'm just too scared to."

He frowned at that. "But you can tell me anything. I promise I won't get angry!"

"And I know that. Well, I hope I do. But I'm still emerging, as it were. Getting out from Kevin's control. He always said I was stupid, and what I did certainly qualifies. I know you wouldn't react like he did, but I just can't tell you. Yet. I will, though. Someday soon."

This seemed to make sense to Trey, which was good, because I wasn't sure it made sense to me. "How about if I stay out in the car while you're at Jesenia's?"

I had to smile at the earnestness in his face. And his persistence. "Okay," I relented.

Trey slipped his arms around my waist, not caring that we were in full view of not only his mother, but also several people out in the dining room who could see us if they peered into the pass-through. He rubbed his nose against mine, a mischievous smirk on his face. "See? That wasn't so hard. But honestly, you can tell me. Whenever you're ready."

"I will."

"Are you two still on the clock?" Gloria sounded more amused than annoyed as she admonished us. She was seated at her desk, reading glasses on, poring over the books, but she paused long enough to frown at us. "Because if you are, smooching isn't in your job descriptions."

"We don't have job descriptions," Trey reminded her.

"If you did, they'd say to smooch on your own time!"

Reluctantly, Trey released me and we went back to work.

JESENIA'S LITTLE cottage was dark, even though it was only late afternoon. All the draperies and blinds were closed, letting in only the smallest amount of light. Her living room, lit only by a single lamp, was therefore full of shadows and dark areas. In the dim light, her collection of frogs looked like unrecognizable black lumps. A cat was perched on the back of the couch, its tail swaying slowly as it contemplated whatever it was cats contemplate. The feline glared at me as I entered, seemingly upset that I'd disturbed its ruminations.

Jesenia's psychic powers must have been working, because she said, "Don't mind Mittens. He doesn't care much for too many people."

I smiled at the cat's name. Mittens seemed so normal a moniker, and Jesenia was anything but normal. She ushered me to sit at the little table she'd set up in the center of the room. A crystal ball was the only item on the otherwise bare table. Staring at it, I said, "It's almost like you knew I was coming."

Jesenia smiled. "I figured you would, sooner or later. About a half hour ago I had a feeling that I should prepare for your visit, so I darkened the room and got everything set up. I'd have felt a fool if you hadn't arrived. But here you are!"

She sat opposite me, and despite her friendly face and warm nature, I found myself wanting to get back up and run out of the house. I fidgeted a little. "I'm not really sure why I needed to see you. You probably can't help me, but—"

"Well, we'll see about that, won't we? First, tell me everything that's happened since the séance."

I filled her in on everything: Kevin's arrival. The fight. My latest sighting of Coleman, and how I'd been possessed, if that was what it had been. The car that had nearly run me over. Several times during the telling of the tale I nearly lost my nerve, and at times I sat for well over a minute, unspeaking and unable to meet her inquiring gaze. During these times she never pressed me, merely waiting until I started speaking again.

I tried to describe how it felt to have another consciousness within me, and how it felt when Coleman had departed to push me out of the way of the car. Words were inadequate, I knew. How could one describe sharing a mind with another person or the sense of, yes, loss when they were no longer there? Jesenia sat quietly and listened attentively, making no comments but offering me encouraging looks when I would pause, not sure if I could reveal the next part of my story. When I was through, she smiled softly and patted my hand.

"That wasn't so bad, now was it?" she asked.

"Says you," I replied with a weak smile.

Jesenia was wearing a flowing light blue outfit with big pockets at the sides. Out of one of these she pulled her tarot cards. "I want you to do something for me. I want you to take just one card out of this deck."

I did so, removing a card from approximately the middle. On it was a depiction of a man and woman, both nude. Presumably they were Adam and Eve, as there was a serpent entwined in the branches of a tree behind the woman. A tree behind the man looked to be on fire. An angel was over them in the sky, hands raised in a blessing.

"The Lovers," Jesenia said. She nodded. "Tell Trey what you've told me. Your future is now melded with Trey's, and he needs to know. See the angel above them? Wearing the purple robe? That's Raphael. The color of his robes represents royalty, and it's a symbol of how important communication is. Tell him. You need to include Trey in what you're doing."

Well, who could argue with a card? I smiled to myself, but I knew I'd take Jesenia's advice to heart.

"Now," she said, settling back, "I want you to look into the crystal. Tell me what you see."

"I thought that was your job. I'm not the psychic, you know." Nevertheless, I peered into the glass. All I saw were refractions of light and distortions of the room around us.

"Oh, I think you've got more than a touch of the vision in you. I believe Coleman has been trying to communicate with people for years, but he's found an affinity with you. He wouldn't have been able to connect with you as he has if you didn't possess some psychic ability."

It was odd. My eyes darted over to the lamp, as I was certain that now there was less light in the room. No, it hadn't changed. But the crystal ball seemed darker to me, almost like it had been filled with smoke. My first thought was that it was some sort of trick, and I passed my hand under the table to feel if there was an apparatus that connected to the base of the crystal to cause this effect. Nothing.

Jesenia must have been able to see the mist as well. "Ah, that's good. I knew you had it in you. Now peer into the fog. See what is hidden."

There were dark shapes in the haze. A man. No, two. I narrowed my eyes, and the mists seemed to clear.

Coleman and Bryan. Naked. In each other's arms. Kissing passionately. And, well, they were fucking.

But then Bryan was no longer there. Coleman was now dressed, wearing jeans torn at the knees, a light blue shirt, and a blue blazer. He was standing in a doorway, which I recognized as the entrance to the Raven's Rest. He was motioning to someone. Me. He wanted me to follow him.

In my mind's eye, I was no longer seated at Jesenia's table. I was in the foyer of the Raven's Rest, and Coleman was beckoning me to join him outdoors.

"Come," he said.

I followed him. He led me down the path to the sidewalk. I tried to catch up with him, but no matter how fast I tried to move, Coleman was always about fifteen paces ahead of me. We went down several blocks until we came to the vacant lot by the record shop.

Suddenly it was night, and I swore I could feel the chill in my bones. The moon above us was partially obscured by clouds. Coleman stood at the edge of the lot, as if he dared not go any farther. He pointed to a spot back by some trees. It was a little wooded area, set away from any buildings or houses. It looked dark and desolate. A person could murder someone back there, and as long as they didn't scream bloody murder, no one would be the wiser.

"There," he said.

"You want me to go back there?" I asked.

He nodded.

I walked past him and began to make my way toward the back of the lot. The grass was high, and it must have nearly been morning, as dew had begun to cling to the stalks. The record shop was dark, as were the houses in the vicinity.

As I got close to the little copse of trees, I could hear sounds, like metal hitting gravel. Someone was digging with shovels or burying something. I could see shadows moving but no details.

Finally I could see the dark forms of two men, bent over a spot of earth, working with shovels. Their task must have been nearly completed, because one of the men moved back and withdrew a handkerchief from his pocket. Wiping his brow, he worriedly glanced around. I must have been invisible to him, for his eyes passed right over me.

"We should have taken him somewhere out of town. The woods somewhere. It was fucking dangerous, doing it here."

The other man was patting down the earth with the back of his shovel. "Yeah? Did you want to get his blood all over the backseat of your car? The little bastard is good right here, right where he is." He paused, peering out of the copse at the closest house, which was a fair distance away. "Believe me, no one saw us."

The moon emerged from its cloud cover, and now I could make out more details. The man mopping sweat from his forehead was Darryl Hollis. He was younger, with no gray in his hair, and thinner than I knew him. I still couldn't make out the features of the other man, who was in the shadows of the trees. I'd heard the voice before, though.

"*Michael, what are you seeing?*" Jesenia was speaking, but she sounded so far away, and muffled, as if I were hearing her from under water.

I couldn't answer her, for fear of breaking the spell I was in. The vision I was seeing seemed so nebulous, so fragile, that the slightest disruption might cause it to shatter. I knew I was sitting in Jesenia Maupin's living room, around a small wooden table, but I was also in a vacant lot in the wee hours of the morning, watching two men with shovels.

And I now recognized the second man. Gary Thornton, the man I'd seen eating with Darryl Hollis at McDonald's. Gary Thornton, who would have been the sheriff of Banning back in the 1980s.

"I know," I muttered. The "me" in the vision, the one standing watching the two men, watched as a fog enveloped the scene. Suddenly I was back, watching a cloudy crystal ball, Jesenia leaning across the table in anticipation.

"You know what?" she asked.

"I know why Coleman wanted me to walk to Trey's last night. I know what he wanted to show me." I sighed and looked up into Jesenia's worried eyes. "And I know where Bryan Finn is buried."

CHAPTER FIFTEEN

WE WERE sitting on the bed in the Ulalume Suite. My legs were splayed out, one on either side of Trey. His were folded, almost in the lotus position. He'd taken off his shoes and was plucking at some lint on his black socks.

"Say something." I couldn't bear the suspense. I'd just revealed everything to him, and while I was sure Trey wasn't going to respond in the way Kevin would have—calling me stupid and yelling and generally playing the martyr at having to put up with me—I still wasn't sure how he'd react.

Trey plucked a tiny piece of fluff off his sock and released it over the side of the bed. It slowly fell to the floor. "Well," he said slowly, not meeting my eye, "first off, thanks for finally telling me. I wondered why you were acting so strange the other day." He scrunched his mouth up and ran a hand through his thick mop of hair. He leaned back a little. "I can understand why you didn't, though."

"It was a dumb thing to do," I said.

Trey shrugged. "Maybe. It turned out to be a good thing, though, if it was Coleman that shoved you out of the way of the car." He looked around the room. "Thanks, dude," he said to the air.

"I don't think he's here right now," I said.

"Doesn't matter. He knows I'm thankful." Trey smiled sadly. "I guess if you were having this conversation with old Uglyface Kevin, he'd be throwing a fit right now, yelling and screaming and calling you names."

"Definitely."

A smile crept across Trey's face. "Good thing I'm not Kevin, isn't it."

"Thank goodness." My heart felt suddenly light as a feather.

"I'd have done the same thing, if it makes you feel any better."

Hell, yeah, it did. "Would you?"

"Absolutely. Coleman's not shown any animosity toward you. I'm the one he scratched, and that was because he was confused, thinking I was making a move on his man. Note that since he was informed that you aren't, despite appearances, his Bryan, he's been a perfect gentleman when I've been here. Well, okay, he made a bit of a mess at the séance, but he didn't harm anyone. Plus, from the sound of it, you weren't absolutely sure of what he was suggesting."

"That's true. But when it became obvious, I didn't put up a fight."

"Might have been too late by then. I think you're beating yourself up over something you didn't really have control over."

Sighing, I leaned forward until my forehead was resting against his. "Thank you," I whispered.

My eyes were closed, but I sensed his smile. "Hey, you're my guy. I gotta stick up for you."

"In my experience, those things don't always go together."

"They do now," Trey said, kissing me just as I moved my head back and was opening my eyes. "Get used to it."

We sat in silence for nearly a minute, gathering our thoughts and holding hands. I looked around the room. "My last night here."

"Yep." Trey didn't sound nearly as wistful about it as I did.

"This is going to sound nuts, but I'm a little sad about leaving without finishing with Coleman."

"You did all you could," Trey told me.

My cell phone rang. It was Erin Hughes. "I'm downstairs" was all she said.

I hung up and nodded at Trey. "You're coming with me for moral support. Right?"

"Absolutely."

We put on our shoes, grabbed our jackets, and went downstairs, where the deputy was chatting with Betty Schultz at the front desk. She paused when we approached, realizing I probably didn't want Lonnie's mother included in our conversation. She excused herself and ushered me and Trey over to an unoccupied corner of the room.

"You were pretty vague over the phone," she said in low tones. "But I gather you've got some information for me, but you can't really say how you got said information."

"Well, I can say," I told her. "You just wouldn't believe me."

"Try me."

"I know where Bryan Finn is buried. At least, I think I do."

She arched an eyebrow. "And how did you come by this information?"

My face was my apology. "I was looking in a crystal ball."

Trey put his arm around me. "I know it sounds—"

"Ridiculous?" Hughes shook her head. "Oh, guys, I've heard worse in my time, believe me. May I ask where he's supposed to be buried?"

"You know that vacant lot down the road? The one toward downtown? There's a patch at the back where there are some trees. He's back there." I was thankful she was still listening to us and not dismissing us outright.

"And you saw this through a crystal ball." It wasn't a question, so I didn't answer. "Let me guess. Jesenia Maupin was somehow involved."

"She was," I admitted.

Deputy Hughes bit her lip. "It's pretty flimsy, guys."

"We know. That's why we called you specifically. At least you know us. You know we're not total crackpots."

"Speak for yourself," Trey muttered to me.

Hughes thought some more, rubbing the back of her neck. Finally she emitted a groan and said, "I appreciate the faith you're giving me, guys, but you have to understand my position here. I can't go to Sheriff Boswell and tell him I've had a great tip and that I know now where a decades-old body is buried because a guy saw it in a crystal ball."

"You don't have to," Trey said. "Michael and I can dig—"

The deputy shook her head. "I'm not sure that's a good idea either. I'm pretty sure that lot is city property, but I'm not completely sure. If someone owns it, you'd be trespassing at the very least."

"Well, we can't just leave him there!" I protested.

Hughes's head shaking became more emphatic. "I can't have you digging holes all over a vacant lot—"

"I know the exact spot!"

She gave me a sympathetic look. "Look, I can tell you're pretty worked up over this. But try to see it from my point of view. Officially, Bryan Finn isn't a murder victim. Most folks around here believe he ran off about the same time as Coleman Hollis back in the 1980s and that they're alive and happy right now. Darryl says he's even heard from Coleman over the years, that he's married and had kids."

"Well, yeah, he would say that. He's the one that killed him." Trey snorted in derision.

Pursing her lips, Hughes seemed deep in thought. "I suppose there's no harm in having the two of you show me the spot."

While it was a concession on her part, it fell short of what I'd hoped for. "It's been decades. It's not like you're going to see anything on the surface after all this time. We have to dig—"

She stopped me, holding up a hand. "Let's just check out the spot and go from there. If I get the right vibe, who knows what I might do? I might feel like doing a little digging. I might not. But I'll check out the area in question."

I managed a smile. "I guess it's better than nothing."

Hughes nodded. "Then you two had better come along and show me the spot. We'd best get a move on, though, while there's still some daylight."

SEEING THE spot in the present, not in a psychic vision, gave me an odd feeling. I knew in my heart that Bryan Finn was buried in the ground under us, but after all the years there was no indication. It was, however, fairly isolated. A huge wooden fence, which, now that I saw it, had also been there in the vision (just a dark shadow there), cut off any view from the north. The trees shielded the area from the prying eyes of the neighbors next to the lot, and a decrepit warehouse was to the east. A person walking along the street might, just might, be able to get a view of someone standing among the trees, but it was unlikely.

Even Hughes had to admit it would make a good makeshift burial site.

"At night," she said, kicking at the ground with the toe of her boot, "you could probably get away with it. As long as you didn't make too much noise." She looked at me. "You need to tell me everything you saw in that crystal ball. Like I said, I can't promise to act on it, but I want to know."

So I told her. This time I included who it was I saw with the shovels. She didn't seem unduly shocked.

"I always had a bad feeling about Darryl Hollis," she said, repositioning her hat on her head. "Nothing I could put my finger on. Just a feeling. Maybe it was growing up in this town and hearing all those stories about Coleman leaving town and never coming back. I think part of me always wondered if he killed those two boys. But Gary Thornton? Never liked the man, but why would he be involved?"

"He was friends with Darryl Hollis. Still is. Maybe Darryl called him, asked him to help out an old buddy," Trey suggested.

"Hell of a favor to ask. 'Hey, I killed a guy. Want to help me bury him?'" Hughes chuckled hollowly.

"Maybe Thornton owed him a favor. A hell of a favor," I said.

Hughes bit her lip and let out a little hiss of air. "You guys have put me in an impossible position," she said. "Officially, I'd have to ignore your information. It's not like I can write on a report that the information came via a crystal ball. I'd be asked to give up my badge."

"And unofficially?" Trey prompted.

"Unofficially, I don't discount entirely that Michael here might have some sort of precognitive abilities. Hey, I'm friends with Betty Schultz, and I'm fully aware that she honestly believes in the ghosts at Raven's Rest, although I've never seen anything myself. But I did see something once that makes me kind of believe this." She looked down at the ground, kicking at the dirt again.

"There was this boy that died when I was in high school. Years later, I was at a party at his parents' house. And I saw him, just for a moment, walking up the stairs. No one else saw it, and of course, people just thought I'd had a little too much to drink. But I know what I saw."

"So you'll check it out?" I asked hopefully.

I was a little surprised to see her shake her head. "No," she said. "I can't. There's just nothing to go on. I have no real reason, other than what can best be termed a hunch, that there's anything here to find." She held up a hand when Trey and I both began to protest. "I said *I* couldn't do any digging. There's no reason you two can't, though."

I looked at Trey. He raised his eyebrows. "I'm sure I can find a couple of shovels."

"You be Burke, I'll be Hare," I said with a wry smile. When Trey and Hughes stared at me blankly, I added, "They were famous grave robbers. I thought everyone knew that."

"Yeah," Trey said slowly, "that'd be a no."

"First let me do some asking around," Hughes said. "Make sure this lot is owned by the city. I'm pretty sure it is. Give me a day or so." Trey and I both made noises of protest, and she added, "If what you think is true, he's been down there a long time. Another day or two won't hurt. Just let me ask around."

Knowing in my heart that Bryan Finn's bones were resting in the ground beneath us, I was conflicted. I knew Hughes was right. It sounded daft, and I could hardly ask her to act on a vision I'd had. But on the other hand, I was itching to prove that, indeed, Bryan Finn was buried here among the trees.

But why was his spirit separated from Coleman's? Why weren't they joined in death? Surely they'd died, if not together, at least on the same day. Or soon after. Had Darryl killed his son's boyfriend first, thinking that would be an end to it? What had really happened all those years ago? Would we ever know for sure? And where was Coleman's body?

I sighed. "You'll let us know as soon as possible, right?"

"Hopefully tomorrow morning. I'll do what I can. You'll be at the inn?"

I shook my head. "I'm moving into my new place in the morning. Got a couch and a bed being delivered and everything. But just call my cell."

Thank goodness I'd taken the day off to move. Now, hopefully, Trey and I would not only be moving furniture but also excavating earth.

In my head I was already hearing my shovel scrape against something that wasn't a rock or dirt, and I shivered.

As it was my last night in the Ulalume Suite, I wanted to spend as much time there as possible, but Trey and I were both starving, so after Deputy Hughes left, we journeyed downtown to a little restaurant that Trey said wasn't "too bad."

It turned out to be a 1950s style diner, complete with red plastic seats (some of which needed repair) and pictures of Elvis and Buddy Holly adorning the walls. We were the only customers, and the waitress didn't seem overjoyed when we arrived. Perhaps she and the kitchen staff were hoping to close up early. When she came, grudgingly, to take our order, she nodded briefly to Trey. "Hey."

"Hi, Suze." He handed her back the menus we'd been handed when we sat down. "Think Bert can manage a couple of burgers and fries?"

"Sure. We're closing in half an hour, though. Just to let you know."

Trey gave her his best grin. "We'll hurry. Promise."

Stone faced, she traipsed back to the kitchen. I waited until she was out of earshot to say, "I hope she's not expecting a huge tip. Talk about service with a grimace."

Trey shrugged. "Not many places in town are open this late on a Sunday night, other than the fast-food places. I guess we should just be happy they're open at all. I went to high school with Suze. She's not bad."

I could have pointed out that she hadn't even glanced my way and had been colder than the water in the glasses she'd brought out for us, but then the bell above the door jangled. "Seems we're not her last customers of the day," I said.

My back was to the door, but Trey's look of alarm made me turn around to see who the newcomer was.

Gary Thornton, the former sheriff, was standing in the doorway. His gaze locked onto mine, and he strode purposefully toward our table. Suddenly I wished the restaurant was a bit more crowded. This man, while possibly not a murderer himself, was at least an accomplice. Who knew what skeletons were in his closet?

Brow furrowed, he stood, blocking any exit I might have wanted to take out of the booth. "What's your game?" he demanded.

I thought about trying to casually take a sip of my tepid water, but I didn't think I could pull it off. My hand would be shaking like a leaf. "What do you mean?" I asked.

"I've been checking up on you," he said, his gaze darting to Trey and then back to me. "Both of you. You've been harassing Darryl Hollis."

"Harassing?" I choked on the word. "I barely know the guy!"

Thornton sneered. "You've been snooping around. Don't think I don't know about it. I've got friends in this town. Talking with that crazy woman, Maupin. Holding séances at the Raven's Rest."

I paled a little. How did he know about that?

"Oh, yeah. Like I said, I've got friends in this town. All this talk of ghosts. Ain't no such thing, and you know it. You're just trying to stir up trouble." He leaned toward me. If he was attempting to be intimidating, he was succeeding brilliantly. "And I'm telling you to stop."

"Seems to me," Trey said, his tone reasonable, "that what we do shouldn't be a concern of yours. You're not the sheriff in Banning anymore. Haven't been for years. You've got no—"

Thornton turned to Trey, his face red and his teeth clenched. "Look, you little shit! I won't have the two of you bothering my friends! Knock it off, before I…."

He let our imaginations fill in the blanks.

I took a deep breath in an attempt to calm my nerves. "We haven't been harassing anyone. We just—"

"You were with that deputy tonight!" Thornton's voice must surely be audible to those in the kitchen. I hoped someone would come out to see what the commotion was about. A witness might keep him from punching either me or Trey, a possible action in Thornton's mind, judging from his tightly clenched fists. "What have you been telling her?"

"You've been following us!" I remembered a car driving slowly along the road as Hughes, Trey, and I had just been entering the vacant lot earlier. I'd paid no attention to the driver, my mind fully on Bryan Finn at the time, but it could have been Thornton. A chill ran through me. Had it been either Thornton or Hollis who had tried to run me down? I'd assumed it had been Kevin or one of his buddies, but now I wasn't sure.

Thornton jabbed a finger in my direction. "If you know what's good for you, you'll leave town. Now. No one wants you here, except maybe this little faggot."

"Hey!" Trey protested. "I'm not that little!"

I admired his ability to be a smartass in a situation such as this. Personally, it was all I could do to keep from peeing myself.

Thornton ignored him, instead curling his lip at me. "Keep your trap shut. That's my advice to you. Stop interfering in other people's lives."

He spun around but stopped in his tracks when I said, "Is there something in that vacant lot you don't want us to find?"

Thornton's face went from beet red to pale white in seconds. I didn't know what made me blurt out the words, but if I'd had any doubt that my vision hadn't been true, the man's reaction proved to me it was.

Thornton turned but this time couldn't meet my eyes. "Stay away from that lot, you little shit. Both of you."

He strode to the exit, but the wind had been knocked out of his sails. There was worry on his face now.

Trey's face bore a look of defiance. "Well, that's got him on the ropes."

"Is that a good thing?" I asked. "He could snap us in two like twigs."

"Hard to do that," Trey replied, "when you're behind bars. There's no statute of limitations on murder."

CHAPTER SIXTEEN

I PUSHED the curtains aside. "Do you think one of them is out there, watching our room? Thornton or Hollis?"

Trey and I were in my room at the Raven's Rest. The television was on, although neither of us was really paying attention to the singing competition show that was on. Trey was lounging on the bed, shoes off, leaning back against the headrest, leafing through a music magazine. "I don't know. Maybe. Can you see anything?"

"Well, no. But from here you really can't see much of the street. They're not in the gazebo, though! I can tell you that!"

Trey grinned at my feeble joke but didn't look up from his magazine. "Any ghosts out there? I hear ghosts like to hang out in gazebos."

"Nope. Quiet tonight."

"They're not in here, are they?" Trey's gaze darted around the room before returning to the article he was reading.

"I don't feel anything."

"Good. I always feel like I'm being watched whenever I'm here. I don't even like to pee when I'm here. I can't help but think Coleman or one of his spooky friends is in the bathroom with me, comparing dick sizes."

I turned from the window and examined Trey's face, which was healing nicely. In another day or so, there would hardly be any traces of Kevin's battering. I knew he was thankful that this would be my last night in the Raven's Rest, but I was feeling somewhat melancholy over leaving.

To get my mind off it, I went and sat down on the edge of the bed, grabbing his right leg and shaking it. "So what ya reading?"

"Article about some young British singer. He's mentioned that he's only nineteen twice in this interview, like it's something special. 'Oh, I'm only nineteen and look what I've done so far!' How the fuck old does he think Mick and Keith were when they started?"

I kept my hand on his leg. God, he was bony. "I wish you'd brought your guitar tonight. You could have played me something."

"I am writing something new. It's still a work in progress, though. Something about a love that lasts even when the two people involved are dead. Can't think where I got the inspiration." Trey tossed the magazine aside. "You're sure Coleman doesn't have his ghostly little eyes on us?"

"Far as I can tell, it's just you and me in the room."

"Good. Then come here."

I scooted up the bed and stretched out until my body was plastered against his, my head resting in the crook of his shoulder.

Trey ran his fingers through my hair and massaged my scalp. "I'm glad you came to Banning," he said.

"Really?"

"Yeah. Despite the ghosts and getting the fuck pounded out of me and being threatened left, right, and center, at least we've got this. We've got each other."

I shifted around, ending up with my head on his chest. He was wearing a T-shirt—black, of course—with the logo of some band I'd never heard of on it. Catfish something. I traced the *C* with my finger, smiling as my touch sent a quiver through Trey's body. The magazine got tossed to the floor. "So what do you want to do tonight?" I asked, now outlining the next letter. Just in case he didn't get the hint, I pressed against him tighter.

"I thought maybe we could play some Monopoly," Trey said. "Or Parcheesi. No one plays Parcheesi anymore. Used to love it as a kid."

I smacked him lightly. "Think again."

He was still running his fingers through my hair and gave a tuft a tiny little yank. "Or I suppose we could get naked and…."

"And?"

"Play strip Parcheesi!"

Like a snake, I slowly crawled up him until our lips could meet. My glasses seemed to be getting in the way of smooching, so they were relegated to the nightstand. Our kisses lingered, and soon I was on top of him.

He smiled contentedly, although I could detect some reticence in his eyes.

"What?" I asked. "Not feeling it tonight?"

Trey rolled his eyes at the impossibility. "No, it's not that. Certainly not you. It's just… this room!"

"I can't sense that Coleman is here."

"Still. This place is creepy. Things you don't see scratch your cheek. Lightbulbs decide to explode. God knows what's going to happen if we start to get jiggy."

I put on my best reassuring face. "Nothing is going to happen, other than I'm going to rock your world. Come on. What's that you told me? Don't let the past control the present."

A grin slowly crossed his face. "It's hard to say no with you squirming like that."

I ground my pelvis against his. "You mean like this?"

Trey put his arms around me and held me tight. Jokingly, he turned his head to speak into the empty room. "Hey! Ghosts! We're going to be busy for an hour or so, and we'd appreciate it if you'd respect our privacy!"

I laughed. "Feel better?"

"I'm feeling pretty good," he said, kissing the tip of my nose, "all things considered."

A thought hit my brain, and I almost told Trey that I loved him. I stopped myself, though. It was too soon. And while my feelings for Trey were strong, there was so much baggage in my emotional life. Leaving Kevin. Finding new work, a new home. Not to mention being involved in a ghostly drama.

"I love you," Trey whispered. Our lips had barely parted.

I looked down into his face, amazed. "I was just about to say that."

"I know."

We kissed again, and our hands began to wander.

We didn't play Parcheesi.

IT WAS nearly midnight when my cell phone rang. Trey and I were still naked, basking in each other's presence, barely covered by the crisp white sheets on the bed. I think I was half-asleep when the call came, and I sat up quickly. I was sure the worry showed on my face. I knew who was calling.

Well, it didn't take a psychic to figure it out. It was late, so it was no casual caller. Gloria was unlikely, as she would have called Trey, even if it was work related. I grabbed my phone and looked at the incoming number. It was Kevin.

My first impulse was to do what I'd done every other time he'd called. I wouldn't answer.

"It's jerkface, isn't it?" Trey asked, almost amused.

"Yep." I started to set the phone back on the table next to my glasses, but Trey restrained my hand.

"See what he wants," he said.

"I can tell you what he wants. He wants me to run back to him with my tail tucked between my legs."

"So this is a good time to convince him that's never going to happen."

I frowned. The phone trembled in my hand. Or maybe it was my hand that was trembling. "You sure?"

"Sure. You can always hang up on his sorry ass if he gets belligerent."

I bit my lip, indecisive, but then answered the call. "Yeah," I said, hoping I sounded tough and resourceful.

"It's me," Kevin said.

"I know. What do you want?"

"Look, I know you're angry with me, but don't hang up." His voice was soft. There was almost a pleading quality to it. After a pause, Kevin continued. "I'm in town. In Banning. I've packed up some of your stuff for you. It's here, in my car."

I was at a loss for words. I stuttered on my reply and had to start over. "I don't know what to say. Where exactly are you?"

"Down in the parking lot. I don't... look, we need to talk."

"I'm not sure that would be a good idea."

Improbable, but it almost sounded like Kevin was crying. "I don't know why you left. I mean, I do but I don't. I don't see that we couldn't have worked things out." He sniffed. "Can we talk? And not on the phone. In person."

"I can't see you alone." The thought terrified me.

"That guy you're seeing. He can be there if you like."

"His name is Trey," I said.

Trey sat up and rubbed my shoulders in a gesture of support.

"Can I see you?"

I'd never heard such pleading in Kevin's voice. Still, I wasn't sure I trusted him.

"Come on in," I said. "We can talk in the solarium. Trey will be close by, though, right in the lobby." I glanced back to make sure Trey was agreeable to this. He nodded.

We agreed on meeting in ten minutes. I hung up with a sigh.

"At least this may give me some closure," I said. Maybe I was being overly optimistic.

Trey continued to attempt to ease my tense muscles. "I'll be right there," he promised.

I smiled, glad my face was turned so he couldn't see. I liked that Trey felt like he was my protector, and in a way, he was. He certainly gave me strength. But we all knew that physically he was no match for Kevin.

I put my hand on his. It was warm and, yes, strong.

Maybe I was selling Trey short. Love could bring out hidden depths. *Just look at what his love has brought out in you*, I told myself.

KEVIN WAS wearing a basketball jersey, his favorite, even though it was getting a little faded and the number, twenty, was beginning to peel away. His jacket, one I'd given him for Christmas, was crumpled on the chair next to him. Appropriate, I thought.

He was sitting in the solarium, his back to the wall, looking at the doorway anticipating my arrival. There were only two lamps lit, so the room was dim, but even in that light I could see his puffy red eyes. He was rubbing his arm nervously when I came in. Kevin had quite a few tattoos, and prophetically, where he was rubbing was one, the word *Veritas* in fancy lettering.

Veritas. Truth. Yes, it was time for a little truth between us.

He forced a smile and half rose when he saw me. "Hey," he said. Settling down again, he added, "I was afraid you wouldn't show."

I sat opposite him in a creaky wicker chair, making sure Trey could see me from his perch near the front desk. He was chatting with Lonnie, but his eyes never left the solarium's doorway.

"I nearly didn't," I admitted. "I had a panic attack while putting my shirt on. Trey calmed me down. Sorry I'm late."

An awkward silence fell between us. Kevin sat forward, wringing his hands. "So you and he are…."

There was no animosity in the statement, so I answered. "He's very special to me."

Kevin nodded. God, he looked sad. "I'm sorry I…." He made a light fist, to indicate the fight. "He's okay, isn't he?"

"He's good."

Kevin examined my face. "And you?"

I touched my lip. "Hardly even swollen now."

Shaking his head, Kevin said, "I've got a bad temper. I know that. It was just seeing you with him…." He realized his voice had started to rise, so he stopped himself. He swallowed hard and then asked, "Why did you leave?"

"You know why."

"I wouldn't be asking if I did."

A faint prickling came over the hairs on the back of my neck, and I had the feeling that Kevin and I were no longer the sole occupants of the room. Had Coleman joined us? One of the other spirits that roamed the halls of the Raven's Rest? Or was it just my imagination? Still, I felt that I was being watched over. It emboldened me, enabling me to continue the conversation.

"We had a toxic relationship," I said. Matter-of-fact tone. No accusations. We were past that. "You were controlling. I allowed you to control me. It got out of hand. I was becoming lost. I didn't know who I was anymore. I had to leave so that I could be me again."

Kevin let that sink in. "We could have worked on it, though. You didn't give me a chance."

"I gave you hundreds. You just didn't see them, or listen to me."

A spark almost caught fire in his eyes. "If you'd have made sense, I would have—" Kevin bit his lip, shaking his head. "I'm sorry. I guess I can't help it."

"No, you can't. It's partially my fault. I let it go on too long. And for that, I'm sorry."

"I never hit you," Kevin said. "Not until the other day."

"No," I admitted. "But your words and actions caused more bruises than your fists might have done. Kevin, I grew to feel that I was worthless. That I was nothing. That you didn't deserve an idiot like me."

For half a second I thought he was going to say that he didn't. But he surprised me by smiling deprecatingly. "The other way around, I think."

Another silence fell. I could hear crickets outside, and the croak of frogs. Hundreds of things came into my head to say, but I quelled them all. Instead I looked at him sitting there, contrite, and for the first time in months I didn't hate him.

"You need to trim your beard," I said.

Kevin chuckled, feeling the scruff on his chin. "Yeah, I guess I do." He leaned forward, his elbows on his knees. He looked into my eyes. I wondered what he saw there. "I still love you, you know."

I nodded. "You'll get over me."

"I doubt it." Never had I seem him so sorrowful. Then he shook off his mood, something he'd always been a master at, and sat up. "So. You're going to stay here. Not come home with me."

It wasn't a question, but I said, "My home is here now. I get my new apartment tomorrow. I'm working at the cafe, and I—"

"Do you still love me?" There was pleading in his face and voice. "At least tell me you don't hate me."

"I don't," I said honestly. "If you'd have asked me even an hour ago, my answer might have been different. But I don't. And I'll always have strong feelings for you. Always. But we can't be together."

"And this Trey guy?" Kevin's gaze drifted over to the doorway, and I was sure he and Trey were looking daggers at each other. I pretended not to notice.

Over a minute went by. It seemed like an hour. Finally Kevin said, "I packed some of your clothes. Figured if you were staying here, you might need some of them. Packed up a box of your books as well. Just some things to tide you over. Maybe sometime you can come up to Rockford and get the rest. I'll behave myself. I promise.

You can even bring Trey with you. For protection." The last was said dripping with irony.

I decided to let it pass. After all, Kevin was being uncharacteristically reasonable. So much so that I said honestly, "I'm glad we had this talk."

"Me too."

I felt the urge to go over and hug him, but I was afraid that might be sending the wrong signals, so I settled for leaning forward and touching him, oh so briefly, on the knee. "I was sure this was going to end up in a yelling match." With him ending up calling me stupid and too dumb to know what was good for me. As usual.

"I guess maybe I should go and apologize to this Trey guy. Unless you think that would be a bad idea."

"No, I think it would be fine." I stole a glance over to the front desk area. Trey was still in conversation with Lonnie. I smiled, seeing him standing as erect as possible and his shoulders squared, ready to rush in if Kevin so much as raised his voice at me.

Right now, it felt great, Trey feeling like he had to protect me. It added to the strength I was finding within myself. But eventually he was going to have to learn, as I was, that I had to stand on my own two feet.

As we left the solarium, though, I looked back for some reason. There, by one of the windows, was Coleman Hollis. Ethereal, barely there, but I could see him, gazing out at the night.

He looked worried.

CHAPTER SEVENTEEN

"OKAY, THAT was weird."

Kevin had driven away more than twenty minutes ago, but Trey still couldn't stop talking about him. Maybe he had worked up so much adrenaline, expecting another fight, that now he had to work off some steam. Trey had accepted Kevin's apology with grace, although it was obvious that the two would never be friends.

The three of us had bundled the boxes (and a hamper full of clothes) from Kevin's vehicle into mine. Tomorrow I'd take them to my new place. Little was said, other than observations about how cold it was getting and me filling Kevin in on my new job. He did make a few sarcastic remarks, but overall he had been on his best behavior.

"He's not all bad," I said, sitting down in one of the chairs in front of the fireplace. Trey had turned on the gas, so a tiny fire was helping to ease the chill in our bones. "I'm really proud of him, in a way. He didn't yell at me once."

"That's because there were other people around," Trey said.

He may have been right. Still, I felt it was an accomplishment on Kevin's part. There had been days when being in a public place wouldn't have fazed him in the least. Trey was pacing, walking from the window to the bed and then to the other chair by the fire. He looked like he was thinking about sitting but then resumed his journey around the room, moving like a nervous cat.

"I think he'd been crying," I said, gazing at the fire. "Kevin never cried. And he was… well, contrite. I think me leaving was good for both of us."

"If you say so. Just don't be surprised if he calls you in a day or two and he's back to his old ways."

"Would you sit? You're making me nervous."

Trey stopped. I was pretty sure he was surprised to find that he'd been roaming the room. Standing by the bed, he made a motion as if he was feeling the air, as if it was a tangible thing. "There's something here. Like you can feel a storm brewing."

"I thought I was the one that was ghost-sensitive." Now that he mentioned it, though, the room did have a charged feeling, like a huge thunderstorm had just hit. Outside, however, the night was dark and quiet.

"Don't you feel it?" Trey was on the move again, at the window, then over to the mantelpiece. "I know something is going to—"

The lights went out.

They didn't explode this time, but I jumped nonetheless at suddenly being thrown into darkness. With a slight hiss, even the gas fire had been extinguished. "What the hell?" I muttered as I sat forward, my heart pounding. Trey was right. There *was* something in the air, a feeling of… anticipation. My head had been so wrapped up in Kevin and his visit that I hadn't consciously noticed before, but now I could feel it. The fine hairs on my arms were bristling, gooseflesh springing up to send a shiver down my spine. The room was much colder than it had been minutes ago as well.

I could see Trey's dim shape by the now dark fireplace. I couldn't see his face, but I knew he was looking at me.

"I don't suppose you can stop this, can you?" he asked.

I shook my head and made a hoarse, stuttering sound before managing to say, "I don't even know what *this* is."

Standing up, I stared in amazement at the corner of the room. There was a light emanating from the very wall, a blue glow that seemed to come from the wallpaper itself, or maybe farther in. It began as a golf-ball-sized spot, but as I watched it grew and expanded until it seemed to fill the corner.

Trey noticed it as well. Out of the corner of my eye, I saw him gaping at the phenomenon. The glow was bright enough now that Trey was bathed in a TV-blue light. "Okay," he said. "That's something you don't see every day."

The glow seemed to take on form, vaguely human shaped. It was now emerging from the wall, like it had stepped through the drywall. Slowly, features became discernible. It was a young man, thin, with white-blond hair. Now I could make out a mouth and a nose. Eyes.

He was smiling sadly. It was Coleman Hollis, of course. In the back of my mind, somehow I had known he'd make an appearance. It was, after all, my last night at the Raven's Rest. How could he not say good-bye?

"You can see him, can't you?" I asked Trey.

"Yeah," Trey whispered. "I'd run and scream, but my legs are shaking too badly."

The spirit became more solid, although he retained his blue tinge. Slowly he moved—glided would be the more appropriate term, as his legs barely moved—toward me.

Trey was muttering under his breath, "Holy shit, holy shit, holy shit...."

"It's okay," I told him. "He doesn't mean any harm."

"He knows that too. Right?" Trey couldn't take his eyes off the specter.

Neither could I, although I felt no fear. Adrenaline was pumping through me, sure, but I wasn't afraid. My body seemed electrically charged, and the tingling feeling increased the closer Coleman came. When he reached out a hand to touch me, I thought I must be bristling with energy. I wondered if my hair was sticking up from static electricity. Hard to tell, as my scalp felt numb.

I put my hand out, and my fingers brushed gently against Coleman's. Instantly he vanished.

Vanished, but he wasn't gone. He was back within me.

I closed my eyes. I could feel him in my mind, stronger than ever. Breathing heavily, I had to hold on to the back of the chair near me to keep from collapsing to the floor. I had to fight the urge to cry out as panic rose within me. The sensation of another consciousness entering my brain, so much stronger than before, was overwhelming.

Just as I began to calm myself, adjusting to the sudden invasion, I heard Trey ask, "What just happened?"

"I'm okay," I said.

"Then why do you sound so strange?"

"Because I'm here," I said. It wasn't me, though. My throat, but someone else was saying the words. I was, in essence, now a ventriloquist's doll. It was odd. I was awake, conscious, but yet I wasn't. It was like I was in my mind, but I was taking a backseat to another persona.

Trey stared at me. "Michael?"

I shook my head. "I'm Cole."

He brought his hand up to his mouth and chewed on a knuckle. "Holy fucking shit," he whispered.

"It's okay. Michael is fine. No harm will come to him."

I was drifting. I could still feel my body somewhat, but it was like I was daydreaming. I could see Trey before me, wide-eyed and looking terrified, but he seemed distant as well. I was reminded of the time I had oral surgery and they put me under. Just before I was unconscious, everything looked hazy, and my groggy eyes saw, but only just. And speech was just too difficult to even contemplate.

Yet I felt warm. Safe. Coleman was speaking the truth. He wouldn't let anything happen to me.

"Michael?" Trey asked desperately. "Don't kid around now. You're scaring the hell out of me."

"Michael's in here," Coleman said. It wasn't me any longer, so I might as well identify who actually was speaking. "He's fine, I promise you."

Trey rushed up to me to grasp me by the arms. "Michael," he said, peering deep into my eyes, "snap out of it!"

"He's okay," Coleman repeated. "Once he regains his strength, he'll be able to talk to you again. But for now, we've got something to do."

"You don't even sound like you!" Trey was shaking. "Come on, Michael! Come back to me!"

"He will. Don't worry. We have much to do, though. I don't know how long I can keep this up. It's taking a lot of energy to do this. Already I'm growing tired."

Trey tugged at my sleeves. I felt sorry for him, but I could tell Coleman was slightly annoyed.

"Shit, Michael! I don't know what to do!"

"There's nothing to do," Coleman said, "except...." He stopped. I think he was still adjusting to talking through me, and he had to pause to reassert himself.

"Except what?" Trey's face was even paler than normal.

"We have to get some shovels," Coleman said slowly.

WE WERE walking down the stairs to the lobby. Oddly, I felt like there were three of us going down the steps, even if there were only two sets of legs. By now I was feeling more aware, although it was a bit like watching a TV show. I had no control over the action. I was but a bystander, impotent and powerless.

"Let me talk to him," Trey said, glancing sideways at me. "You'll just creep him out."

"What?" Coleman asked. "Why are you staring at me like that?"

"Your hair. It looks straighter somehow. Less curly."

"It's just your imagination," Coleman said, although I could sense that he wasn't entirely sure Trey wasn't right. Was Coleman's essence being within me causing physical changes as well? Was my hair becoming more like Coleman's? If he remained in my mind, would my eyes change color again? Had they already?

Best not to think about such things. A panic attack wouldn't help me, and probably not Coleman.

Luckily, Lonnie Schultz was still manning the front desk. He looked half-asleep, perched on a stool, a book lying open on the desk before him. He nodded at me and Trey when we approached. "Hey. What's up, guys?"

Trey motioned for me to stay a few feet back while he went up to talk to Lonnie. He leaned against the counter and spoke in a low voice. "We need a favor," he said.

"Yeah? Anything I can do. You know that."

Trey gave him his most ingratiating grin. "You wouldn't happen to have a couple of shovels we could borrow, would you?"

BY THE time I was sitting in the passenger seat of Trey's car, I was almost entirely myself again. Coleman was still in there, but he had used up too much energy. Now I was just getting vague impressions from him, words and thoughts here and there, like a radio not quite tuned in to a station properly.

"What did you tell him?" I asked.

Trey slammed his door shut and glared at me. "I told him we had a burst pipe at my mom's house and there was some garden damage. Don't ask me why we had to replant the posies in the middle of the night, or how the pipe burst in the first place. It was a lame excuse, and Lonnie didn't buy it, but we got the shovels. I could hardly tell him that we were going to go dig up a body that's been buried for over thirty years." Trey's eyes narrowed. "I'm assuming that's what we're doing, right?"

"It is. Pretty sure, anyway."

As he turned the key in the ignition, he kept his eyes on me. "Who am I talking to right now?"

"It's me, Michael. Honestly."

"And Coleman?"

"He's… resting."

Trey's nerve seemed to leave him, and he threw his head back, banging it against the headrest. "This is too freaky for words."

I touched his arm. "It's going to be okay."

"He's in you still, though?" Trey was almost whispering. "What does it feel like?"

I thought about it. "I've got a bit of a headache, and I feel a little sluggish. Like just then, when I reached out and touched you. Normally you just reach out and do it, but I had to stop and think about it, if that makes any sense. Like when you're really drunk and have to concentrate to do simple things. It's really hard to explain."

"Yeah, I bet. He knows he can't stay there, right?"

"He knows."

Trey put the car into gear with a sigh. "Might as well get this over with. I'm assuming we're going to the vacant lot."

"No."

"No? But I figured—"

"Just drive, Trey."

"It would be nice," Trey said as he pulled away from the curb, "if I knew where I was going."

There was no traffic. No one was out taking their dogs for a late-night walk. The town seemed deserted. The night was cloudy, and the wind had picked up. A couple of drops of rain spattered against the windshield. I stared ahead, although I was also seeing brief images flashing in my mind, which I assumed was Coleman, trying to tell me where to go. "You know that road by the old Baptist Church?"

Trey frowned. "Cedar Road? That doesn't go anywhere! When they put in the new bridge, they closed that road. It's a dead end!"

"I think that's where he wants us to go."

"You're freaking me out. You know that, right?"

"This is the end of it," I said. "It's hard to explain, because I only get flashes of Cole's thoughts and memories, but I can tell he's been working up to this. It's taken him a while to figure out just how to communicate with me, how to use his energy correctly. At first he was very confused and frustrated, but now he knows how to get me to see what he wants me to see."

"Which is?"

My smile was thin. "I guess we'll find out when we get there."

We were now going down Lincoln Boulevard, which is one of Banning's main drags, so it wasn't out of the ordinary that there was a car following us, but my heart seemed to beat faster when I noticed the headlights in the side-view mirror. Two o'clock in the morning. It could just be someone coming home from one of the bars. Banning certainly had a lot of them for a small town. It worried me just the same.

"Do you think that guy is following us?"

Trey hadn't noticed the car, but he squinted now into the rearview mirror. "Could be. Want me to do a James Bond and shake him?"

"Just don't get us arrested."

We were approaching one of the few traffic signals in town, so Trey timed his speed so that he barely squeaked through the yellow. I twisted around to see the other car run the red light to keep up with us.

"Not conclusive," Trey noted, "but suspicious. I mean, at this time of night, I'd have done the same thing. Stop when there's no traffic? But it could also be either Darryl Hollis or Gary Thornton, keeping tabs on us."

Trey took a right turn, hard enough that the safety belt was the only thing that kept me from being thrown against the door. "What are you doing?" I asked, readjusting my glasses. They'd slipped down my nose from the jolt.

"Just taking a little detour to make sure. He still following us?"

"Um… no." There were no lights in the mirror, but I turned to look back to make doubly sure. "I can't see anything."

"Might not have been anything, then," Trey said, visibly relaxing. He made a few more rapid turns, basically taking us around the block to get back on track. When he turned onto Lincoln again, there was no sign of any moving vehicles.

We came to the edge of town, where there was a used car dealership, a medical clinic, an apartment house, and not much else except for the Banning Baptist Church, sitting on a hill by the woods. Here Lincoln Boulevard actually became Riverview Road, a winding path that led to the highway to Rockford. Trey, however, turned onto Cedar Road, just past the church.

The road wasn't in the best condition, and Trey slowed considerably as he dodged potholes. "The town officials were going to put a chain across here to keep people from using the road," he told me, "but people still come down here to fish."

The car lurched as we hit a particularly large hole. "I'm guessing they're not going to fix it up, then."

Once past the church, the road actually got worse. There were some outbuildings on our left, storage spaces for, one assumes, whatever wouldn't fit into the church basement. On the right was a dense, thick woodland. The wind had picked up, and rain now hit the windshield with more frequency, causing Trey to turn on the wipers.

"Lovely night," he grumbled.

"This is the right place, though," I said, looking out at the trees as they loomed, dark and ominous, seeming to close in on the slow-moving car.

"We won't be able to drive much more. Soon we'll come to the…."

The headlight beams lit up a barricade ahead of us, with a Bridge Out sign attached. Trey stopped the car but kept the engine running. He peered out at the spectral limbs hanging over us. The area illuminated by the lights was dismal and forbidding. Everything else was murky blackness.

"You brought flashlights, right?" I asked.

"Yeah. Like they're going to help a lot." He pointed at the bridge, although I could only make out its vague outlines. "The last time I was down here, and mind you, I was in high school at the time, this bridge wasn't in the best condition. I'm sure it's worse now. We'll have to be careful going across. Assuming, of course, that we're supposed to be on the other side."

"We are. We need to head into the woods."

Trey watched the rain fall. "I'm going to be cold. I'm going to be wet. And, unless the shovels are just for atmosphere, I'm going to be sweaty. Is there anything about this I'm going to like?"

"You'll be with me."

He grudgingly accepted this. Trey sighed as he shut off the motor. Opening the car door, he muttered, "Let's get this over with."

Trey, a gray (not black!) beanie clamped onto his head, went around to the trunk. I donned a baseball cap (Trey's, and it had Foo Fighters World Tour on it) and joined him. As I waited for him to find the release catch, I gazed around me. Trey was right. It was chilly, rainy, and with the car lights off, dark as hell.

Trey finally found the release, but as the trunk swung open, he paused and looked behind him. "Did you hear that?"

I looked back down the road, not that I could see much. "Just the wind," I said. The sky rumbled. "Thunder?"

"It wasn't that. And I thought I saw a light. Way back there."

"We might be able to still see the lights of the town from here. Maybe you caught a glimpse." I hoped I sounded convincing, because I wasn't sure I believed it. I shivered, yearning for a warm blanket, a safe, dry room, and a cup of hot chocolate. "Give me one of those flashlights, would you?" I couldn't take the eerie darkness much longer.

He handed me one, as well as a shovel. We both flicked on our beams and scanned the area. Trees. The bridge loomed over us. My flashlight couldn't break through the gloom to show me all of it, but it revealed enough that I wasn't exactly eager to try my way across it. The girders were dark with rust, and the deck, wooden beams, had rotten sections that I could see myself falling right through.

"Shaggy and Scooby-Doo wouldn't even head over that thing," I said.

Trey didn't argue the point. "Let's go. Keep to the sides and we should be safe enough."

Awkwardly, I held the shovel and flashlight in the same hand. I wanted a free arm to reach out and grab hold of a girder if the rotten wood under me decided it wasn't going to hold my weight. Trey went first, moving carefully. He was halfway across before I'd even made it a quarter of the way. Well, it's hard to make your way across a broken-down bridge when your knees are knocking, your heart is racing, and your head is swimming. Finally I paused, mostly to readjust the shovel and flashlight, but also to wipe the rain off my chin.

Trey noticed I wasn't moving and turned his beam my way. "You okay?"

"Not really. I'm a little dizzy."

"You've passed the worst part. Honestly. You can do it."

I walked a few more paces before stopping again. Shaking my head, I said, "I'm not sure I can do this." I looked over the side of the bridge. Blackness. I had no idea how high up I was. I didn't think it was horribly far, but I still had a touch of vertigo. "What's this bridge over? A river?"

Trey laughed. "Just a ravine. Probably was a stream at some point."

My flashlight was pointed down at the deck in front of me. Trey was just a phantom voice floating in the darkness. I tried to continue but ended up holding on to a rusty support beam with my free hand. "I can't do it."

"You're doing fine. Here, I'll come back and help you."

"No, it's my head. I—"

I sank to my knees, and the shovel clattered onto the deck. Somehow I managed to keep hold of the flashlight. I felt sick and rubbed my forehead, dislodging the baseball cap in the process. It tumbled off my head, hit the wooden boards, rolled, and went over the side into the abyss.

"I lost your hat," I said miserably.

"Fuck the hat," Trey said. He was closer now. I sensed he was only a few feet away, but my eyes were shut tight, so I wasn't sure.

"I think it's Coleman," I said. Maybe he was experiencing intense emotions at being here, and they were affecting me. For I was sure Coleman had been here before. Hell, I was sure he was buried not far from where we were. Why else would we be out in the middle of the night armed with shovels?

I felt Trey's hand on my shoulder. "What can I do?" he asked. "Here. Let me help you up. I'll lead you across."

I bowed my head in agony. Gritting my teeth, I said, "I think I'm going to throw up. I—"

And suddenly the feeling passed. Another took its place, though. I gasped as I felt the headache leave me, but my sinuses and mouth seemed like they were full of a dusty smoke. As I sat there on the wet, rotten boards, a misty stream burst from between my lips and out of my nostrils. The foggy strands met and shot forward, forming a cloud that quickly moved across to the other side of the bridge until it disappeared into the darkness.

Trey watched the phenomenon in awe. "Was that…?"

"Yeah. He's out of me." I blinked. Yes, Coleman was gone. I was totally myself again. Slowly, with Trey's help, I got to my feet. "I'm okay," I told him.

"Yeah, I'm sure. People have another personality residing in their noggin all the time. Careful! You're still shaky."

I had made a little lurch but grabbing the girder kept me upright. "I guess I'm still a little woozy."

Trey asked worriedly, "Do you think you can make it? I can go on my own, you know. I'm sure old Coleman will show me where he wants me to go. You can stay in the car."

I shook my head. I really was feeling better by the second. "No, I'm good."

Trey had dropped his shovel when he'd rushed to help me. Now he bent over to retrieve it. Looking off into the trees, he said, "I can just see a little glow in there. See it? I'm pretty sure we're supposed to follow old will-o'-the-wisp."

I followed Trey's gaze. Through the rain, I could just see a faint glow in the gloom ahead. "I think you're right."

Armed again with our lights and shovels, we slowly crossed the bridge. It seemed to take an eternity, but it probably wasn't more than five minutes before I was on solid ground again. I wasn't even aware that I'd been holding my breath until I finally stepped off the deck onto the road. Trey was right by my side, and he flashed me a grin.

"You did it!"

I didn't really feel like celebrating. We still had a trek ahead of us, I assumed, and I was chilled to the bone and soaking wet. "Let's just get this over with."

Just to add to the mood, right then there was a flash of lightning and a peal of thunder.

Trey pointed with his flashlight toward the spot in the woods where we'd seen the glow. It was no longer there. "I think that's where we're supposed to go. There doesn't seem to be a path."

If I thought traversing the bridge had taken forever, our journey through the woods was just as bad. The going was tough, and our shoes were soon coated with mud. The terrain was uneven, and I slipped twice, falling on my ass, getting my jeans muddy as well as wet. My bones, already sore from nearly getting run over, protested with each tumble. Every now and then, we'd catch a ghostly glow emanating from between some trees ahead of us—Coleman's way of keeping us on track, I supposed. At one point, Trey led the way through a thicket of bushes, pushing branches out of the way as he went. One branch whipped back, scratching his face. We paused to assess the damage.

"Just a little blood," I assured him, shining my light on his cheek.

He touched the wound with his grimy fingers. "Figures I'd find a way to mar my face even more."

I started to say something, but the sight of a pale figure ahead of us stopped me. Coleman Hollis's spirit was standing at the edge of what seemed to be a ravine, watching us patiently.

Trey noticed him as well. "I think we're there."

The ghost nodded and then pointed down into the ravine.

"That's where it is," I said. "That's where Coleman's grave is located."

Chapter EIGHTEEN

THERE WAS a place where the incline leading to the ravine was just barely manageable, and Trey and I tossed our shovels down first before we attempted to make our own descent. It was messy going, as the rain was now pouring down, making the ground soggy and hard to find a good foothold. A young sapling growing sideways out of the incline helped, as Trey and I both grabbed hold of it to steady ourselves.

By the time we reached the bottom, Trey was coated with mud. I was sure I was the same. He tried to wipe some of the grime off his leather jacket, with little success. I'd already decided that everything I was wearing was going straight to the garbage rather than try to clean it.

I removed my glasses and tried to wipe away the rain. It was futile. "I don't see Coleman anymore," I said, "but I can still sense he's near."

Trey looked around us. The ravine had likely once been a stream, probably running down to the Rock River. Now it was just a gully. Trey played his flashlight beam over the rocks, stumps, and sodden ground. "I wonder where we're supposed to dig."

I stood near a large stone. "Right here."

"You sure?"

I felt it in my bones. It was the right place. "Yes."

We took turns digging, although Trey was much better at it than I was. I'd either try to slice the blade too far into the ground and then find I couldn't shift it, or I'd end up with only a quarter of a shovelful of earth. We'd made a fairly good hole in no time, though, thanks to the soft ground.

"You sure this is the right place?" Trey asked, tossing clumps of mud off to the side.

"Positive."

Trey paused, looking up at the top of the ravine. "Shine your light up there."

I did, although I could see nothing.

"I thought I heard something," Trey said.

"An animal, maybe?"

Trey shrugged. "It may not have been anything. It's easy to spook yourself out here. I can't imagine why."

He slammed the shovel blade into the ground but then paused. "What's that?"

I crept closer to our hole, and the flashlight picked up something dirty white in the mud.

"It's a bone," I said.

WE UNCOVERED most of what we decided was a leg before figuring we had what we wanted. Trey tried to call the sheriff's department, but there was no signal.

"Let's head back into town," he suggested. "We can take Deputy Hughes out here, or whoever is on duty. They can do the rest of the dirty work."

Now that we were finished, of course, the rain began to dwindle. I looked up. There was no glowing figure. There hadn't been since we'd uncovered the bones. I wondered if the discovery had brought an end to Coleman's ghostly existence. If so, that made me slightly sad. Despite everything, I'd miss him. We had, after all, bonded in a way that few people could ever claim.

Eyeing the muddy slope before us, I asked, "And just how are we supposed to get back up?" We'd mostly slid down on our butts. Well, I had.

"We'll leave the shovels down here and get them later, for one thing," Trey said.

"They aren't ours."

"Who's going to steal them? A beaver?" With a sigh, Trey braced himself for the climb.

Several times I decided we weren't going to make it. On my first attempt, I didn't get very far. I got maybe two feet up when a clump of dirt I was using as a handhold came loose and I stumbled back, nearly ending up on my ass once more.

Trey fared better. He grunted as he grasped the trunk of the little tree growing out the side of the incline, which was about the halfway point. There was a snapping sound as one of the branches came off in his hand. "It's not so bad once you get this far," he said. "More footholds."

Actually, it looked worse, but I kept my doubts to myself. My flashlight tucked in my armpit, I tried again. "I hate nature. Have I told you that?"

By the time I got to the little tree, I was exhausted. I held on to that little sucker for dear life. I could see Trey ahead of me, hauling himself over the ledge. He turned and extended down an arm. "Just get close enough and I can haul you up."

"I weigh more than you!"

I couldn't see his face as I was unable to point the flashlight beam properly with it in the crook of my arm, but I knew he was beaming encouragement at me. "You can do it, Michael!"

The sapling made a cracking sound as I tried to haul myself up farther. I looked back down to see just how far I'd fall if it gave way. Dawn was just beginning to break, and I could make out a little. The drop wasn't huge, but there was a big old rock right below me, and I certainly didn't want to slam against that. If I broke a bone, I'd have to wait until Trey went to get help, all the while knowing a body was buried just a few feet away.

That thought spurred me on. I scrambled up the side of the hill, finally getting to where I could grasp Trey's outstretched hand. He helped me haul my weary carcass over the edge. Just before my legs swung onto solid ground, I dropped the flashlight. It hit against the rock and the light went out as we heard the glass break.

"The sun's coming up anyway," Trey said.

It was true. I could not only see him, but could make out some details of his face as well.

We sat near the edge of the ravine for several minutes, catching our breath. Trey and I exchanged glances.

"You're filthy," I told him.

"So are you. And your glasses are crooked."

The lenses were smeared with mud anyway, so I left them as they were. "At least now I'll be able to see going back over that fucking bridge."

"Yeah. You ready? Let's get going."

We stood but didn't move. Behind us a twig snapped, and we heard a shuffling sound.

Turning around, we saw Darryl Hollis emerging from behind a tree. "What are you guys doing out here?" he growled.

"You followed us!" Trey accused.

Hollis didn't answer, but I figured Trey was only half-right. Hollis hadn't been there the whole time. Otherwise he'd have stopped us from digging up the bones of his dead son. So he must have just arrived. Maybe someone reported to him that they'd seen Trey's car go down Cedar Road. That would be enough to get him to come out and investigate, and he'd know just where to check.

"We found the body," I said, hoping my fear didn't show in my voice. "It's over. We know you killed your son and Bryan Finn. Bryan's buried in the vacant lot. Your son is here."

Although it was getting light, Hollis was still far enough away that it was hard to make out his expression. Was he angry? Despondent over finally being found out? All I knew was that my adrenaline was pumping.

It went into overdrive when he took a step closer and I could see that he had something in his hand. He was holding a tire iron close to his side.

Hollis noticed that I'd spotted his weapon, so he held it up. "Normally I don't go anywhere without my gun. Wouldn't you know it, the one time I forget it is the time I really need it? But I figured this would do the trick just as well."

"We don't want any trouble," Trey said, his voice shaking.

"You asked for trouble when you dug up my son's body." Hollis began slowly walking toward us, his grip on the tire iron tight.

I gulped. "You can't get away with killing us. Deputy Hughes knows what we're doing. No one will believe that Trey and I ran off like they did with Coleman and Bryan."

Technically, Hughes didn't know that we were out in the wee hours digging up a body, but she knew enough that Hollis would come under immediate suspicion if we went missing.

I wasn't sure, by Hollis's face, that he was listening to reason. There was a snarl on his lips as he brandished the iron, ready to bring it down on my skull.

I started to back up and realized in time that I'd only go over the edge into the ravine. Bringing up an arm to ward off the blow (fat lot of good that would do!), I cried out and moved to the side, knowing I probably wouldn't be able to dodge the blow entirely.

Trey shouted, "You fucker!" and dove at Hollis. He didn't reach him in time, but it threw Hollis off enough that the iron hit me on the shoulder and not my head.

I fell, yelling in pain and clutching my left arm. I was only inches from the ravine's edge, and my feet were dangling in the air. Vaguely, I saw Trey trying to tackle the bigger man. He knocked him off balance but not off his feet. Hollis swung again, but as Trey was plastered to his side, the best he could do was to smack the weapon against Trey's back. He got in two good hits.

It was enough. Trey went down, moaning. He tried to hold on to Hollis but ended up sliding to the ground holding on to the man's leg. Hollis kicked Trey off, and Trey rolled onto his back, his face contorted in agony. Still, when Hollis attempted another kick, Trey made a grab for the man's foot.

Hollis shook himself free and gave Trey one more kick to the side before returning his attention to me. Trey was pretty much out of it, holding his side and groaning.

I shifted, giving myself more space between me and the edge. Hollis loomed over me, the tire iron held high. He was blurry, and I realized my glasses must have fallen off when he hit me the first time. "You little fucker," Hollis snarled. "Couldn't leave well enough alone."

"*Daaaad!*"

The sound could have been the wind, but I knew it wasn't. Hollis must have as well, as he paused, the tire iron still ready to slam into my skull.

"*Daaaad!*"

Darryl Hollis turned his head. Standing a few yards away from us was the ghost of his son, Coleman. Coleman wasn't solid, but you could see him well enough. The long blond hair, the sad green eyes.

"Cole?" Hollis's voice was uncertain.

"Don't do it, Dad."

Hollis's lips quivered. "You're dead," he said flatly.

"Dad, please!"

Hollis shook his head. "You're not real. You can't be." He turned back to me, murderous rage back in his eyes. "This is all your fault, you little bastard! You've got me seeing things!"

He started to bring the tire iron down.

I only half saw what happened, because I had shut my eyes to brace for the blow. I was aware that the wind had picked up, as it whistled in my ears. When I dared to open my eyes just a little, wondering why Hollis hadn't followed through, I realized it wasn't the wind I was hearing. Coleman Hollis had vanished, at least his form had. In his place was a fog, a mist. It was this, rushing toward Darryl Hollis, that caused the cacophony.

Hollis didn't see the ghostly cloud until it was upon him. His eyes opened wide in fear, and he screamed as he stumbled back to get away from the rapidly advancing mist.

And he tumbled over the side of the ravine.

As he disappeared, the spectral fog vanished.

I heard him fall. I heard the thump of his body hitting the ground, but I heard something else as well. A cracking sound. A sickening thud, and I knew even before I peered over the edge that Darryl Hollis's skull had hit the big rock at the bottom of the ravine.

I twisted so I could see better. He was sprawled out in the mud, and sure enough, his head was lying on the stone. Blood was seeping out of the back of his skull, staining the surrounding area.

With a groan I rolled onto my back. "Trey?" I asked. "Are you okay?"

"Peachy," he answered. "You?"

"I can't move my arm. Damn, that guy is—was—strong."

"What happened? Where is he?"

"He fell over the edge. If he's not dead, he soon will be."

"Can't say I'm horribly upset over that. Guy was fucking insane."

I wasn't going to argue the point. I smiled, despite the pain in my shoulder. Here we were, just having escaped being murdered, lying in the mud having a chitchat. "Shouldn't one of us call the cops?"

Trey fished his phone out of his pocket. After a moment I heard him snort. "No signal."

I got mine out, but the result was the same. "I guess we'll have to walk."

"That should be fun," Trey said.

Somehow that made us both laugh like idiots.

Chapter NINETEEN

"MICHAEL, HONEY?"

I was in the kitchen of the Coffee Cafe, preparing some sandwiches. It wasn't easy going, as I had to do it mostly one-handed, as my right arm was in a sling. The lunch rush was over, but we still had a few customers. I looked up to see Gloria Ramsey speaking through the pass.

"Yeah?" I thought she had some changes the customers had made to their order.

"Deputy Hughes is out here. She'd like to have a word with you. Trey can finish those up."

Trey overheard and was already gently pushing me out of the way, smacking his hip against mine. "Move," he said jokingly. "You're in my way."

I stuck my tongue out at him and went out to see what Hughes wanted.

It had been days since the police had uncovered the bodies of both Coleman Hollis and Bryan Finn. Finn had actually been buried in an old trunk that Darryl Hollis and Gary Thornton had hauled out to the vacant lot. Gloria had reveled in the gossip as it trickled into the cafe.

Earlier, Trey's mother had filled me in on the "consensus of opinion" from the gossipmongers of Banning. "Apparently," she said, in that hushed tone people use for the really juicy tittle-tattle, "Bryan Finn was the first victim. Darryl Hollis spied the young man leaving his son's bedroom late one night and followed him outside. The two got into an argument, and Hollis beat and strangled poor Bryan. Then he got his buddy Thornton to help him bury the body."

While I was certain something of the sort had taken place, I wasn't sure Gloria had the facts correct, and I must have shown my skepticism because she assured me she got her "intel" from Betty Schultz, who had heard it from Erin Hughes herself.

"See, Darryl thought that if he got rid of Bryan," Gloria went on, "there might be a chance for Coleman. I guess Darryl thought he could beat Cole into being straight. Cole became suspicious, though, and Darryl lured his son out into the woods and killed him. Buried him right there, where you found those bones."

I suppressed a shudder, thinking about that night. I was sure I'd have nightmares about bridges, bones, and storms for months to come. At least in the dreams I'd had so far, Trey had been there to offer comfort and solace.

I also wondered what stories Gloria had spread about that night. So far, from what I heard, Trey and I had been barely alive when we finally crawled across the abandoned bridge. One customer asked me if it was true that Trey had left me barely conscious in the woods while he went back to the road and flagged down a passing car. I assured her that the story was exaggerated.

The truth was considerably less dramatic. In fact, we'd both made it over the bridge, and we *had* tried to get a couple of cars to stop for us, but the drivers had sped off, undoubtedly thinking that it wasn't in their best interest to pick up two ragged, filthy guys in the early hours of the morning. Trey and I had laughed at the face of one motorist as he increased his speed at the sight of us.

Back on the road, though, we finally had a phone signal and called the sheriff's department.

I went out to the dining room to find Hughes seated at the table by the front window. She smiled and stood when she saw me.

"You're looking well," she said, shaking my hand.

"Better than the last time you saw me, anyway." Hughes had been one of the deputies who had responded to our call. The other officer had been dubious when we said we had found a body out in the woods, or maybe he just hoped we were wrong. "You guys sure it was a human body? People hunt out here all the time," he'd said. "Maybe it was the bones of an animal." Hughes hadn't doubted us for a moment.

"You got time to sit?" Hughes asked me.

I looked back to the counter, where Gloria nodded. Hughes and I sat.

"I thought someone should bring you up to speed about what we've found." Hughes looked tired, probably from working extra hours. A decades-old double murder wasn't exactly something the town of Banning dealt with on a regular basis.

"I've heard that Gary Thornton confessed his part in the crime," I said.

Hughes's cheek twitched. "I really can't talk about that, although, just between you and me, his lawyer has warned him that he's said too much already. No, what I wanted to tell you was about Bryan Finn. Or, more accurately, about the box he was buried in."

"What about it?"

"It was a very old chest, lined with metal. Might be lead. I don't know. Tin is more likely, I'd say. But Jesenia Maupin stopped me on the street this morning, and she said she had a vision about Finn's burial."

I sat forward. I knew better than to dismiss Jesenia's visions.

"She said that the metal lining of the box must have held Bryan's spirit there. Inside the trunk. That's why, according to her, Bryan and Coleman's spirits couldn't be together." Hughes sighed. "Of course none of that goes on any report I'll be making. I just thought I'd let you know."

"Thanks for telling me."

Hughes tilted her head and went for a change of topic. "How's the arm?"

I wiggled the fingers of my damaged appendage. "Painful. But I guess it was a pretty clean break. The doctor's putting the cast on tomorrow. He wanted to wait for the swelling to go down. Luckily, he gave me some awesome pain pills."

"And the new apartment? Settling in okay?"

"It's fine. Perfect. Still feels a little weird, living on my own. But I think I like it."

"Well, you're a Banning resident now. Officially."

I grinned. "I'm not sure, considering the things that have happened, if that's a good thing or not." I spied Trey working back in the kitchen. At least Banning had him going for it. That was enough to keep me in town, if nothing else.

"Jesenia also told me that you and she are going back to the Raven's Rest later on today. Another séance?"

"Not exactly. It was Betty Schultz's idea, actually. She wants to see if the spirit of Coleman Hollis is still in residence, or if he's gone now. Jesenia's just going to see what her psychic impressions tell her."

I was anxious to see what the atmosphere of the inn would be as well. Was Coleman at peace, finally? I hoped so.

"ARE YOU ready for this?"

Trey sounded chipper, the words offhand and easy, but I knew there was a seriousness behind them. I felt so close to Coleman Hollis. Hell, he'd been literally a part of me! What if all that I'd—we'd—gone through, had all been for nothing? What if Coleman's spirit was still trapped within the walls of the Raven's Rest, doomed for eternity to be searching for his lost love?

"As ready as I'll ever be," I said, sighing.

An early snow had started to fall. Big, fluffy flakes filled the air, and I was reminded of an old Peanuts cartoon, which had Charlie Brown, Lucy, and the gang attempting to catch snowflakes on their tongues. Maybe that would be a better way to spend an evening, out in the open air with Trey and trying to relive childhood glories. Better than a night in a haunted inn, checking on the status of its resident ghosts.

Trey held my hand as we mounted the porch steps of the Raven's Rest. It was comforting, which he meant, but also natural. Trey was my rock, my anchor. Unlike with Kevin, though, I didn't feel like Trey defined me. I was a person on my own. With Kevin, my only identity had been Kevin's boyfriend. That was my existence. My fault as well as Kevin's, I know, but it had become so toxic. With Trey, I was me. Trey's boyfriend, yes, but more as well.

That was an empowering thought. Slightly terrifying too, but I could deal with it.

What I wasn't sure I could deal with was what lay beyond the inn's front door.

Inside, I was surprised to find that nothing seemed to have changed. I had thought—hoped, even—I would immediately sense that Coleman's spirit had gone, happy that he'd finally been reunited with Bryan. But standing in the foyer, I couldn't tell. The atmosphere seemed the same. Lonnie was behind the desk, chatting with some guests. He smiled at us in acknowledgment before returning to the couple obviously checking in.

"Well, if it isn't Banning's favorite couple!" Jesenia Maupin emerged from the solarium, wearing a bright blue outfit with lots of frills, her Town Witch button proudly situated over her breast. The couple at the desk turned in puzzlement, but Jesenia ignored them. She swooped over and gave Trey and me a kiss on the cheek in turn. After kissing me, she turned back to Trey and pinched his cheek. "And this one's so handsome, I could just eat him up!"

Trey blushed, touching his face. "Um… yeah. Thanks." There were still slight traces from where he'd been scratched that night in the woods. The bruises on his back from being clobbered by Hollis had been nasty-looking, but the damage was actually slight, as the man couldn't really get a good angle. Trey assured me that they didn't really hurt, although I'd caught him swallowing some ibuprofen before we'd headed out.

The new guests gathered up their bags and headed for their room. As soon as they were gone, Betty Schultz entered. I had the feeling she'd been in the solarium waiting for them to depart. Probably didn't want mention of ghosts in the inn to put off new arrivals. She beamed at us as well, and she was holding a copy of the *Banning Herald*. The front page was devoted to the big story, complete with pictures of the places where Coleman and Bryan had been buried, and shots of Hollis, Thornton, Trey, and me.

I'd already seen the paper and cringed at the thought of the photo of me and Trey. It had been taken as we'd left the sheriff's office, and I hardly thought it was flattering. I thought I looked like death warmed over. Trey, however, looked scruffy and ragged but still somehow managed to be handsome as hell. Or maybe that was just my prejudice showing.

"I should have you autograph this," Mrs. Schultz said, tucking the paper under her arm. "You've certainly given us a boon. We're almost full up!"

"People wanting to stay in the haunted inn?" Trey asked.

There had been no mention of ghosts in the newspaper, but Jesenia had written a long blog post about our experiences. Word had apparently gotten out.

"Mostly," Mrs. Schultz admitted. "Some are just staying here because of the notoriety of the murders. I've already had two calls from reality TV shows. You know, those true ghost type shows. Something tells me we won't be having a slow period for quite some time!"

Jesenia touched my arm. "Betty has kept the Ulalume Suite free, though, so that we can check it out."

"Have you been up there yet?" I asked.

She shook her head. "We were waiting for you. Betty's been in there, of course, and she says it seems pretty quiet. I'm not sure, though." Jesenia gazed around her. "I'm still getting a weird vibe about this place. I know Coleman wasn't the only spirit haunting the inn, but I'm getting the impression that he's still here. It's faint, but my instinct so far tells me he hasn't moved on."

That disappointed me. I had hoped we'd helped Coleman.

Lonnie had been listening in to our conversation. "Personally, I'm kind of hoping he's still here," he said, wearing his usual cheeky grin. "Life was interesting when he was around!"

Jesenia wiggled a finger in his direction. "Oh, don't you worry. There are other spirits roaming this old place. One little girl called Lisa has been talking to me since I came in here! And she's got a crush on you, Lonnie, so you just watch out!"

I had no idea if Jesenia was kidding the young man or not, but his face grew serious. "What? A ghost has the hots for me? What the hell! She's not watching me, you know, in the shower or anything?"

Jesenia didn't answer him but merely smiled slyly. To the rest of us, she said, "Shall we go upstairs now? I'm anxious to get the feel of the room!"

The four of us traipsed up the stairs and made our way to the room I had so recently occupied. Mrs. Schultz had a key card ready, but we all paused at the door, almost reverently.

"I don't know about anyone else," Trey said, "but the hairs on the back of my neck are doing the Watusi."

Jesenia placed her hand flat on the door panel. She shook her head. "I'm getting a faint trace of him," she said, her eyes closed in concentration. "Maybe it's just a residual impression, since his presence was so strong here. I can't tell."

Mrs. Schultz made a sour face. "Well, we're not going to find out anything by lollygagging out here."

She opened the door.

I didn't know what I had been expecting. Maybe a burst of ghostly wind to come rushing out at us or the room bathed in a spectral blue hue. Instead, as we entered and Mrs. Schultz turned on the lights, we were met with a simple, quiet room.

Walking to the bed, I said, "I'm not getting anything myself."

Jesenia tilted her head. "I feel... something. It's faint but there."

"Shouldn't we do something, you know, like asking old Coleman if he's still around?" Trey asked. "Get him to speak up if he's still around? Maybe hold another séance?"

Mrs. Schultz's face brightened. "Maybe we're in the wrong room." We all looked at her as she went on to explain. "This wasn't Coleman's room when he was alive. The Raven Suite was. If he's anywhere, wouldn't he be in the place he was most comfortable?"

"Can we go there?" Jesenia asked. "Is it occupied?"

"It's booked, but they haven't checked in yet. As long as we don't spend too long in there...."

Moments later we were entering the Raven Suite. As soon as I stepped over the threshold, I could feel a change in the atmosphere. When Mrs. Schultz switched on the lights, I almost expected to see Coleman sitting on the bed, awaiting us. The room, however, was empty. At least of visible entities.

Jesenia agreed with me. She spun around, arms outstretched, soaking in the environment. "He's here!" she announced. "I can feel him!"

"He hasn't moved on," I whispered, moving over to the bed. I touched one of the pillows. "Why hasn't he moved on?"

"Something is keeping him here, even still," Jesenia said. "Maybe...."

She may have let the sentence drop, or maybe she kept on talking and I just didn't hear her. Suddenly I wasn't completely with them in the room. It changed for me, the furniture and surroundings shifting before my eyes. I grabbed the bedpost, feeling dizzy. Finally the change was complete, and I was seeing the room as it had been back in Coleman's day.

But weirdly, I was aware that Trey, Jesenia, and Mrs. Schultz were still with me. I could see them, hazily, but I knew they weren't seeing the room as I was.

Coleman was sitting on the bed, speaking into a telephone. He was alive, real. Not a ghost. I knew this, although I had no idea how I knew it. I was having a vision of some sort, a glimpse into the past. It was now 1983, and Coleman was wearing a tight white sleeveless shirt and shorts. He seemed worried as he spoke into the receiver.

"But Mr. Finn, I haven't seen Bryan for days." Coleman's eyes were welling with tears. "Please, if he's there—" He listened for a moment. "Okay. If he comes in, please tell him to call me right away."

If I reached out to touch Coleman, to offer him some comfort, would he feel it? Was I just a shade, watching but helpless to interfere, like Scrooge when shown events from his youth by the Ghost of Christmas Past? I sat on the bed. It felt real. And I could smell Coleman's cologne.

I looked back, and Trey, Mrs. Schultz, and Jesenia were standing together, watching me with interest. Jesenia's mouth was moving, but I couldn't hear the words clearly. Something about me being in a trance and that they shouldn't disturb me. I turned back to Coleman. He had hung up, and he clutched the phone to his chest, his face in agony.

The door opened and Darryl Hollis entered. He was younger than the Hollis I knew. There was no gray in his hair, and he had less of a gut. "I thought I told you to stay off the phone," he growled.

"I've got to find Bryan," Coleman replied, putting the phone onto his nightstand. "I know—"

"I don't want you seeing him. I told you that." Hollis's voice was hard, cruel. "You're better off without him, and the sooner—"

"I don't want to be without him!" Coleman shouted, rising to his feet. His cheeks were flushed with anger. "I love him! And you can't do a fucking thing about that!"

The effect of this outburst on Hollis was frightening. He stepped forward, his hands clenched at his sides. There was murder in his eyes and countenance, and I shrank back instinctively, even though I was sure he couldn't see me sitting there.

"No son of mine…," he began.

"Oh no. No son of yours could be a faggot." Coleman's lip quivered, and he chuckled mirthlessly. "You're pathetic. I hate you. And I'm not staying here another day."

"Leaving town is probably the best thing for you," his father said, snarling.

Coleman shook his head. "Oh, I'm not leaving. I'm going to go stay with Marshall, at least until Bryan and I can get up enough money to get out of here. I know you'd rather have me out of your sight entirely. Can't have the town know that your only son is a flaming homosexual. Well, guess what, Daddy darling? They're all going to know. I'll make sure of that."

Darryl Hollis picked up an ashtray. A big, heavy glass one. The remains of a joint and several cigarette butts went flying as he raised it high over his head.

And then he brought it down onto his son's skull.

I BLINKED. I was no longer in Coleman's room, but now in a car. An old model Buick, but it looked fairly new. Hollis was driving. It was dark, and we were turning onto the road by the church. I was in the passenger seat, frightened by the man sitting next to me, even though he seemed unaware of my presence. There was a tiny moan from the backseat, and Hollis growled, "Just sit tight. We'll soon be there." He seemed to think he was saying something funny, because he chuckled. It wasn't a pleasant sound. "I'd bury you with your little friend, but there's not room for two in that trunk. That, and it's just too dangerous. I can't believe Gary talked me into burying him in that lot. Sure it was out of the way, but… right in the middle of town. No, we'll take you out where no one will find you."

We were heading over the bridge. While it still looked rickety to me, it at least looked like it would hold the weight of an automobile. Outside, the moon shone down, bright and stark, as if in judgment of Darryl Hollis and his actions. It was an angry moon, holding him in contempt.

I turned. Coleman was bundled into the back. It was hard to see him, but he looked half dead. Blood was running from a wound on his temple, dripping down onto his face. His eyelids fluttered, and I wondered if he knew where he was and what was happening. Had Coleman died in pain?

I felt a gentle hand touching my elbow. "Michael? Are you okay?"

It was Trey, his eyes full of concern. I shook my head, and the car, the bridge, poor Coleman, and his father were gone. I took a deep breath and realized I was crying. Wiping my cheeks, I said, "Yeah. I just… I just had a vision."

Jesenia asked softly, "What did you see, honey?"

"I saw it all." I sat on the bed, feeling suddenly weary. "I saw Darryl Hollis kill Coleman. I saw him drive out to the woods. Coleman was in the backseat. I think he was still alive at that point, but only barely. I saw—"

I put a hand up to my temple. Flash. In my mind, I saw a shovel striking earth. I saw Darryl grunting as he piled the dirt aside. The hole he'd made was nearly ready. Coleman's body lay off to the side, eyes open, the blood drying on his face. Oh, so dead. Oh, my God. What a waste. How pointless.

Flash. Darryl Hollis and Gary Thornton, sitting in a restaurant. I didn't recognize it. They were huddled over coffee cups, talking low.

"It's over," Hollis said, unable to make eye contact with his friend.

"You convinced him to leave town?" Thornton asked.

Almost imperceptibly, Hollis shook his head. I had the impression that what I was seeing was the morning after he'd killed his son, but it could have been days. The man looked like he'd aged overnight. His eyes nearly had a sadness in them. "I... he's out in the woods. No one will find him."

Thornton didn't answer right away. He looked around, making sure no one could overhear their conversation. "Maybe it's for the best. We'll just say they ran off together. I'll talk to Martin Finn, make sure he won't kick up a fuss. Doubt if he will. We'll convince him his son up and left. Martin's a good buddy. I'll get him to believe that Bryan met some boy and they took off together. People in town are already pretty sure that boy is queer." He spat out the last word.

"Without any of his belongings?"

Thornton smiled. It wasn't a pleasant smile. "We'll make it work. The guy he met had money. We can make him a sugar-daddy type. Hell, Martin will be happy we took care of his problem for him. Janice I'm not so sure about."

Hollis set down his coffee cup and stared at his hands. The hands of a murderer. "I didn't mean to do it. I just lost my temper."

"Of course you did. Who wouldn't? Those boys were sick, perverted. Believe me, you've done the world a favor. Darryl, this is a small town. You couldn't put up with people talking behind your back, could you? Having a son that's a fruit? No, this is best. After a month or so, you can tell people you've heard from Cole, and that he's living out in New York City or someplace. A year or so from now, you can tell people he's gotten married. Together, we can spread enough rumors that people will think he's still alive and well. And not a fucking faggot."

"Yeah." Hollis sighed deeply. "Maybe you're right."

"MICHAEL?" TREY shook my shoulder. He was sitting next to me on the bed. I hadn't been aware of him at all while the scenes had played out in my head.

I looked at him sadly. "I saw everything. Darryl Hollis strangled Bryan Finn. I'm not sure he meant to do it. He lost his temper. A day or so later, he killed his own son. Hit him over the head with a glass ashtray and then buried him out in the woods. All because Coleman and Bryan loved each other. No other reason. Just because of love."

Trey put his arm around me and pulled me close. I cried into his shoulder, letting it all out. Betty Schultz and Jesenia stood by, silently. As my sobs began to subside, a look came over Jesenia, as if she heard something. She moved over to the window. Looking out, she gasped.

"Michael, come over here, quick!"

I wiped my nose using the sleeve of my sweater and stood slowly. Once I was sure I could walk without my knees giving out on me, I joined Jesenia at the window.

Outside, the moon was shining down brightly. The stars were out. But that wasn't what Jesenia wanted me to see. Down by the gazebo, I could see two misty figures. They were in a sort of blue glow, but I immediately recognized them as Coleman and Bryan. They were holding hands and looking back at us. Coleman had a tear running down one cheek, but I could see the happiness in his face. He was beaming, oh so happy. He looked lovingly at Bryan and then back up at us. He waved.

Mrs. Schultz had joined us at the window. "Oh, my Lord," she muttered.

The figures turned and began to walk off. With every step they took, they became more and more indistinct. After several yards, they vanished altogether.

"What? What's going on?" Trey was attempting to see, but the three of us were blocking his view. "What's out there?"

Jesenia smiled at him. "They're together now. They're at peace." She took in a deep breath, holding out her hands. "Oh, yes. I can feel it now. Coleman's spirit has departed. There's nothing keeping him here any longer. He's been reunited with his love."

Trey finally wedged himself in between me and Mrs. Schultz, but there was no trace of the spirits remaining. "They were out there? Both of them? And I missed it?"

"They're happy now," Jesenia said.

"Yeah, I'm glad for that. I really am." Trey was peering out, hoping to catch just a glimpse. "But I went through a lot for those two, and I don't get to see the big good-bye? That kind of bites. I hate to say it, but the least they could do—"

I kissed Trey on the cheek. "I'll make it up to you, handsome."

Betty Schultz sighed. "Well, I guess that's that. I don't suppose we'll see Coleman's ghost hanging around the Raven's Rest anymore."

"No," Jesenia agreed. "He's gone for good."

"I wonder if…."

She didn't finish, because at that moment the door to the room slowly creaked open.

I could see nothing, but apparently Jesenia could. Maybe her psychic abilities were more finely tuned than mine, or maybe I was only able to see Coleman Hollis because of the connection between us, me resembling Bryan Finn so much. Jesenia smiled at the empty doorway.

"Welcome," she said. "And you are?"

Chapter TWENTY

Next to me in bed, Trey stirred.

I rolled over so that I could look at his face. He was still asleep, his face calm and relaxed. No scratches. They'd faded to oblivion weeks ago. He looked so sweet lying there, not brooding or coming up with some sarcastic comment. I could see what he must have looked like as a child. There was so much innocence in that face.

He groaned, shifting position. Now his nose was buried in his pillow, his long hair falling over his eyes. Mumbling something unintelligible, he lazily brought up a hand to rub his chin.

After two weeks of living on my own, I caved and begged Trey to move in with me. I just couldn't take the silence. To be fair, it hadn't taken a lot of begging. One night he'd come over and I'd cooked him spaghetti. I had one glass of wine too many and got a little maudlin. He comforted me, cuddling with me on my brand-spanking-new couch.

"What's wrong?" he asked.

"I don't like living alone. Move in with me."

I felt, in a sense, like I was letting myself down. Giving in. My independence over. My discovery of myself over.

On the other hand, I knew Trey was no Kevin and that our relationship would be far different. In the end, I just knew I wanted to have him around all the time.

Besides, he *really* needed to move out of his mother's place.

He shrugged. "Sure."

The nonchalant act he'd tried to put over failed when, right after dinner, he'd gone home to pack and had returned less than an hour later, laden with boxes.

"I'll get the rest of the stuff tomorrow. Which drawers are going to be mine?"

He couldn't fool me. Half of his boxes (at least) had already been packed, in readiness of me asking him to move in with me. I was just glad that a chest of drawers had been added to my list of things to buy.

Now I watched him as he woke. One eye opened slowly. He brushed the hair out of his eyes to get a better look at me. "Morning," he said, his voice gruff.

"Morning," I said, kissing him on the cheek.

"Were you watching me sleep?"

"Maybe."

"Pervert."

"You love the attention, and you know it."

He lifted his head off the pillow just enough so that he could see the pack of cigarettes sitting on the nightstand. I knew he wanted to light one up, but when he moved in I'd insisted that he couldn't smoke in the apartment. It had been our first and, so far, only argument. He obviously was aching for a nicotine fix, but he'd have to get up, put some clothes on, and go out in the chilly November air. So instead he turned so that his back was to the nightstand and kissed me on the lips. He gave me a little bite as he pulled away, maybe to show his annoyance at my "ridiculous" rule. I just smiled.

"Give them up," I said, knowing he knew what I was referring to.

He smiled a little sadly and put his arm around me. "I'm not as strong as you are."

That surprised me. "You think I'm strong?" To me, he was the one with all the strength. Any I had, as I saw it, came from my love for him.

Love. That surprised me as well. Scary, but it was true. I loved the long-haired, guitar playing, Man in Black Johnny Cash wannabe that was Trey Ramsey.

"Sure you are. All that stuff with ghosts and murders and digging up bodies? Most people would have freaked. Hell, I bet most guys would have run right back to Kevin, despite him being a controlling bastard—"

"He's trying to be better. By the way, he called yesterday. He said we can go up to Rockford and pick up more of my stuff anytime we want. He even has some furniture we can have, as he's getting some new stuff. We'll have more than a couch to sit on."

"Yeah, I'm sure he's suddenly a saint." Trey wasn't going forget losing that fight with Kevin anytime soon. "My point is, 90 percent of dudes would have run screaming the first time they saw Coleman's ghost. You didn't. You helped him."

"And he helped me." I saw Trey's point, though. Maybe I had more strength than I gave myself credit for. A glance at the alarm clock, sitting next to Trey's cigarettes, told me we didn't have time to discuss it further. "We'd better be getting dressed. Jesenia will be here any moment."

Trey rolled his eyes. "Let's just ignore her when she knocks. We'll have sex instead."

I fixed him with a mock angry glare. "She's a psychic. She'll know we're in here."

"So? I—"

"And she'll know what we're doing."

He thought about that a moment. "Okay. You win. I still think this little ceremony of hers is silly."

"It's for closure."

"For whom? Coleman and Bryan? They're gone, aren't they? For us? I don't know about you, but I'm willing to put the whole thing behind us. Turn the page, fresh chapter." Trey continued talking as he slipped out of bed. He was naked, as he never slept with anything on. I admired his cute little butt as he struggled into some boxer shorts. God, he was lovely.

Me, I was in the pajama bottoms that I normally wore. I always slipped them on after our nearly nightly bout of lovemaking while Trey threw on just enough clothes to survive going out for his last cigarette of the day. These clothes would be hastily discarded, scattered about the room, when he climbed back into bed. Neatness, thy name is *not* Trey Ramsey.

"Oh, hey, did I tell you? Mom's planning a vacation next month," Trey continued as he dressed (all in black, naturally). "Yeah, and she says she's thinking of leaving me in charge while she's gone. Ain't that a laugh? Me, in charge of people. God, I can only imagine what shape the cafe will be in by the time she gets back. She's going to Italy, of all places. Anyway, she's showing me how to do the books later, so I may have to leave right after Jesenia's little shindig...."

He kept up the chatter, and I began only half listening. I already knew about Gloria Ramsey's vacation plans, and more. A few days ago she'd revealed to me that she was slowly grooming Trey to take over as cafe manager on a permanent basis. She'd just stay on as the bookkeeper but was planning on working far fewer hours.

"I want to get back into gardening! I want to take trips!" she'd told me during a slow period. Trey wasn't working that day. "Do you know how many hours I work here a week?" I had a good clue. A lot. "Now, if you'd asked me months ago if Trey could take over running this hell hole, I'd have laughed. But he's changed a lot. I credit you with that, Michael. He's not the lazy smartass he used to be. Now he's a motivated smartass. I think he wants to show you he can succeed. Just keep him from painting the whole place black, will you?"

I had promised to keep her plans for Trey secret for now. She didn't want to shock him into returning to his indolent ways.

As it turned out, we'd have had ample time for morning sex, as Jesenia was horribly late when she arrived. She flew into the room, a flustered vision in blue, speaking before the door was hardly even opened.

"I know I'm late, but I had to do some extra meditating to prepare for today."

"By which she means she overslept," Trey muttered so that only I could hear.

We bundled into my car, and we quickly made the trip to the Raven's Rest. It was still odd seeing the inn now that I no longer stayed there. In a strange way, it still felt like home. I wondered if that was a residual feeling from Coleman Hollis.

Erin Hughes, Betty, and Lonnie Schultz were there on the porch, waiting for us. Everyone was wearing heavy coats since the temperature had steadily fallen for the last several days. Soon the lawn would be coated with snow, and reindeer and Santa decorations would replace the skeletons and witches that had overseen the lawn when I'd first arrived at Raven's Rest.

The six of us quickly made our way over to the gazebo, the place where I'd last seen the spirits of Coleman and Bryan. We stood, roughly in a circle, waiting for Jesenia, who was rummaging in a big paper bag she'd brought with her.

"Do you feel anything?" Trey asked me quietly. "They still here?"

I shook my head and looked at Jesenia for confirmation. She'd pulled a little red book out of her bag, and she smiled at me. "I don't feel them either. They're gone, and they're happy now. That damned box they buried Bryan in! The metal lining kept his spirit prisoner! Really, people should know better!"

I doubted if, while burying Bryan Finn, Darryl Hollis and Gary Thornton cared much whether or not they were keeping Bryan's spirit separate from that of his lover.

Jesenia opened the tiny volume and read several prayers. I wondered what the book was, as they certainly weren't Christian prayers, although they were lovely. When she'd finished, she turned to me. "If you would do the honors, Michael."

I found the cross Trey had made in Jesenia's paper bag. The bottom end had been fashioned into a stake to make it easy to stick it into the ground. Well, that was the theory, anyway. The ground was hard, though, and I had trouble with getting the cross deep enough that it would stay put. Finally, with Lonnie's help, we got it far enough into the dirt that it wasn't going to be uprooted by a strong wind.

We all looked at it in silence. Trey held my hand. Finally Erin Hughes said, "I hope they've finally found peace."

"They have," Jesenia assured us.

Trey nodded solemnly. "Good-bye, you two. It was an adventure."

Written on the crossbeam were these words:

Coleman Hollis
Bryan Finn
Together Now Forever

STEPHEN OSBORNE has been a pizza restaurant manager, a semiprofessional wrestler, and a member of an improv comedy troupe. He now lives in rural Illinois with Christine, a Border terrier mix with a diva complex. In addition to writing, seeing musicals in Chicago, and losing at Monopoly, Stephen sometimes spends cold, shivery nights in haunted locations—just because he likes to.

Facebook: www.facebook.com/stephen.osborne2
Twitter: @southbendghosts
E-mail: leftyIN@yahoo.com

Pop
Goes
the
Weasel

Stephen Osborne

Patrick Weasley, aka Weasel, is a fun-loving college student with a wealthy homophobic jerk stepfather and a best friend, Jake Winston, who's just as gay as Weasel. When Jake's aunt dies, many from the publishing world—including Jasper, Weasel's weasel of a stepfather—gather at Winston Manor for the reading of the will, and Weasel is obligated to tag along.

Turns out all he has to do is three things: 1) swap the wills so Jake's uncle inherits the house instead of the gardener, who's also an old enemy of Weasel's; 2) secure a publishing contract from author Cecily Talbot; and 3) hook Jake up with his deceased aunt's male nurse. But what he ends up doing is 1) falling for Tony, one of the food servers; 2) accidentally affiancing himself to Cecily; and 3) fighting with Jake, who thinks he was making a play for the nurse.

To make matters worse, every time Weasel and Tony start to get intimate, Jasper is right around the corner. So when burglars come to steal a valuable piece of art, Weasel must 1) use all his ingenuity to keep the painting safe; 2) dis-engage himself from Cecily; 3) unite Jake with the nurse; and most importantly, 4) pursue Tony to an elusive happy ending.

www.dreamspinnerpress.com

Stephen Osborne

Speaking
of
Dreams

When it's meant to be, it's useless to fight it.

Four years ago a drowning accident brutally ripped Jason out of artist Frank Hunter's life. As he celebrates his forty-fifth birthday with his friends, Frank knows his dating life is over. A chance meeting with Donny Rodriquez, however, shakes Frank's world to its core. Donny is twenty years Frank's junior, but so full of life and vitality that Frank knows he has to paint the young man. Donny agrees, although he makes his romantic interest in Frank plain. Frank does his best to put Jason and the past behind him, but the memory of his late lover won't let him go.

Yet Donny sparks something in Frank, and after several disastrous dates with men his own age, Frank ends up back with Donny. Donny soon learns that to win Frank's heart, he must not only bridge the age gap but find a way to enable Frank to let go of the past.

www.dreamspinnerpress.com

STEPHEN OSBORNE

WRESTLING WITH JESUS

Bookstore owner Randy Stone is smitten. His new boyfriend, Kyle Temple, is sweet, hot, attentive, and great in bed. But introducing Kyle to his family takes courage, because Randy's parents can be a little judgmental, and Kyle is ten years younger than Randy, a small-time pro wrestler, and dumber than the proverbial sack of hammers. Needless to say, Randy's parents aren't exactly thrilled, and even his best friend is skeptical.

Despite the challenges, Randy is determined to tough it out for Kyle. After all, enduring a few scornful comments from his mother is nothing compared to what Kyle's going through trying to quit smoking for Randy. When a hypnotherapy session designed to help with Kyle's cravings leaves him quoting Jesus Christ—in Aramaic—Randy's parents are suddenly the least of their problems. Once word gets out, their privacy is destroyed. News crews follow them everywhere, and everyone who knows Kyle seems determined to make a buck. It's a mess that could make Kyle's dreams of wrestling in the UWE come true—but what about his dream of being with Randy?

www.dreamspinnerpress.com

PALE AS A
GHOST

STEPHEN OSBORNE

A Duncan Andrews Thriller

Private detective Duncan Andrews's best friend Gina is a witch. His dog is a zombie. And his dead boyfriend, Robbie, is a ghost. So it's hardly any wonder that he uses his connection to the supernatural to help him solve cases. Good thing, too, because Duncan has his hands full. Janice Sanderson, the richest woman in Indianapolis, wants him to find her stripper daughter, Brenda, and another client is having some trouble with a specter haunting her family home. On top of that, Duncan has decided to add dating into the mix, though after Robbie's death, he's not sure he's ready.

When Duncan meets Nick while tracking down a lead on Brenda's boyfriend, he shelves his doubts and agrees to a date. Robbie doesn't make it easy on him, showing up to spoil his chances, but that is the least of Duncan's worries—because one of his clients' husbands is missing and there's a serial killer on the loose—one Duncan fears isn't human.

www.dreamspinnerpress.com

ANIMAL INSTINCT

STEPHEN OSBORNE

Sequel to *Pale as a Ghost*
A Duncan Andrews Thriller

Private detective Duncan Andrews has the home-team advantage when it comes to solving paranormal crimes: His best friend, Gina, is a centuries-old witch. His dog is a zombie. And his boyfriend, Robbie, is a ghost.

Duncan certainly has his work cut out for him with this case. Someone's been using the skull of a powerful wizard to control animals, and whoever it is, they're not out to set up a petting zoo. For Gina, the case hits close to home—she knows just how dangerous it is, since the wizard was her father.

Just when he thinks they're close to breaking the case, tragedy strikes, leaving Gina in a coma. Then, after years as a ghost, Robbie finally decides to move on, leaving Duncan to protect young Ashton Marsh, the victim of several strange animal attacks. Suddenly Duncan is working without his supernatural safety net. Without his friends, can Duncan defeat the power of Eleazar's skull and keep Ashton alive? Or will the struggle for his life end in broken bodies as well as broken hearts?

www.dreamspinnerpress.com

THE
SCARLET
TIDE

STEPHEN OSBORNE

Sequel to *Animal Instinct*
A Duncan Andrews Thriller

Duncan Andrews, a private detective who specializes in paranormal cases, is back, along with his usual gang. Robbie Church, his boyfriend, is a ghost. Gina, a centuries old witch, is his best friend. And Daisy, Duncan's bulldog, just happens to be a zombie. Odd man out seems to be Nick, a history teacher. He's a normal, living human.

Duncan's latest case leads him to a rock band in Indianapolis called The Scarlet Tide. It doesn't take Duncan long to realize all of the band members are vampires. He sets out to destroy them, but runs into trouble with the charismatic leader of the band, Dominic Hunt. Duncan ends up under Hunt's psychic control, and is forced to examine his relationships with Robbie and Nick, as well as his attraction for Hunt. Can Robbie and Gina help Duncan break Hunt's psychic grip? Is there any hope the vampire can be destroyed once and for all?

www.dreamspinnerpress.com